New Market Tales

Jayant Kripalani is an Indian film, television and
stage actor and director. He is best known for his
performances in television series such as *Khandaan,
Mr Ya Mrs* and *Ji Mantriji*. He graduated from
Jadavpur University, Kolkata with a degree in
English Literature and has worked in the advertising
industry before moving to film and television.
New Market Tales is his first book.

New Market Tales

Jayant Kripalani

PICADOR INDIA

First published in the Indian subcontinent 2013 by Picador
an imprint of Pan Macmillan, a division of
Macmillan Publishers Limited
Pan Macmillan, 20 New Wharf Road, London N1 9RR
Basingstoke and Oxford
Associated companies throughout the world
www.panmacmillan.com

ISBN 978-93-82616-06-1
Copyright © Jayant Kripalani 2013

Typeset by

Printed and bound in India by Replika Press Pvt. Ltd.

For Gulan
Without whom…

Francis

At the south end, the posh end of Free School Street is Park Street, where all the restaurants and nightclubs were. Trincas on one side, Sky Room on the other; with Kwality's, Moulin Rouge, Blue Fox, Olympia, Magnolia's, Oasis, In and Out at The Park, and Flury's, in between and on opposite pavements. Many have come and gone. There might have been more – I forget. But I do remember they were all there in a quarter of a mile stretch of glittering lights.

We used to watch the patrons going in and out of the clubs and restaurants (we were too young and couldn't afford them). Often we'd watch the nightclub artistes going in, and drool. I remember Dawn who used to sing at Trincas, she was advertised as 'Deadly Dawn' on the posters. All of us, full of pre-adolescent fantasies, would dream about 'waking up at the crack of Deadly Dawn.'

At the other end of Free School Street was Corporation Street which, not surprisingly, housed the offices of the Calcutta Municipal Corporation in a gigantic Victorian edifice that smelt of old files, stale sweat, and fresh piss. In between Corporation Street and Park Street were pimps, brothels, seedy hotels, drug peddlers, a fire station, The Armenian College, auctioneers, a butcher who had the finest goats on offer, a kite-wallah who sold the most lethal manjha in the city (second only to the kind I used to make), and St Thomas School with a church attached.

Right opposite the church were music shops where you could buy an old Perry Como 78 rpm record if you were inclined that way, and of course second-hand bookshops that threw up treasures every now and then – Balzac and Maupassant second editions presented to *My darling James Bartholomew Jones – from Patricia, his ever-loving wife. March 1879* in exquisite calligraphy.

It was here in 2009, on a nostalgia trip to Calcutta, that I discovered a dog-eared copy of *Winnie the Pooh* presented to me by my neighbour and friend, Francis. The inscription inside read: *To my best friend, Raju. Happy Birthday. August 14, 1962* – written in a childish scrawl.

Someone, in my absence, a caretaker or a friend had been raiding the overflowing bookshelves of my unoccupied home, selling my books. I bought my book back.

I crossed the street and walked into St Thomas Church. It was empty. Peaceful. But not restful. I looked up at Francis' god. 'Why did Francis have to die just two years after he'd given me *Winnie the Pooh*?' I asked.

Naturally, I got no reply. After all, this was the Protestant Jesus and Francis was a devout Catholic. Perhaps I could shift to a Catholic church and ask the same question.

Francis was the baker's son who'd sworn that he wouldn't eat a loaf of bread again. But I'm rushing ahead of my story.

Everything about Francis, above the waist, was fat. He had a fat neck which was connected to a fat head, a fat chest and tummy, and all this fat was parked precariously on long, spindly legs. He also had the longest fingers you would have ever seen – fingers that could spin a cricket ball round the legs of the finest batsmen we ever played against. The YMCA team we defeated regularly were determined to whisk him out of our team into their's, strictly on religious grounds. 'I am a marketayr bachcha,' he said proudly. 'I'll play for the New Market XI on Calcutta's grounds.'

Every morning at six, we used to go practice at the nets. I'd pick Francis up from his bakery-cum-home at the corner of Colin Lane and Free School Street. Walking up to his house every morning was sheer joy. His father, Augustine D'Costa, baked the finest breads in Calcutta. And the area was resplendent with the smell of fresh bakes. Rumour has it that people would take a bus ride from the southern-most tip of Calcutta, a ride that took an hour and a half in a state-run bus, just to collect a loaf or four from Augustine's.

One of those mornings, I walked to their house to pick Francis up. I always walked in through the back gate where an old Austin A40 was parked. It was polished maroon, with varnished wood panelling. The seats had been removed, and replaced with racks to carry bread, muffins, patties and pastries to the D'Costa's shop in the last row of the New Market.

Francis, and a very surly Francis I might add, was loading the first tray into the van.

'Hi Francis,' I said.

'Humph!'

'Now what?'

'Shut up, Raju. Just give me ten minutes, and I'll be with you.'

'Let me help. We'll finish in five.'

He just shrugged and walked back into the house. I followed him in.

Augustine, his father (and there was absolutely no doubt that Augustine was his father – same neck, same head, same proportions) stood next to an oven, yes, on his spindly legs, his face gleaming with sweat and joy. He was the happiest when he baked. His wife Miriam, with her back to the door, was elbow-deep in dough, punching it and pummelling it as she spoke.

'He's started telling lies (*punch*). He lied before, but now ... (*a bit of serious knuckle-work on the dough*) ever since he started going out with that Raju fellow, that jeweller's son (*two quick, violent punches*) ... he has been evading me. And he's become stubborn. Lies and stubbornness!'

Ninette, Francis's sister, and Augustine, had noticed our entry. Miriam hadn't. It was one of those inexplicable moments when everybody was embarrassed for everybody else.

'I'll go get my kit,' Francis said, and left the kitchen in a hurry. Miriam paused her kneading, noticed me, and punched the dough even harder than before.

'I could die for the smell of freshly baked bread every morning ... Hello all,' I said trying to lighten the mood in the room.

'Here, have a croissant,' said a much-relieved Augustine, handing me heaven on a paper napkin. 'Even the French can't make it better.'

Disgusted by Augustine's polite gentleness, Miriam pummelled the dough a bit more.

'Aunty Miriam, are you annoyed with me?' I asked.

'Yes, I am,' she glowered at me.

Normally Aunty Miriam had the kindest of eyes. They looked benignly at you and out at the world. The only other time I had seen so much venom in them was when Kanwaljit from the neighbouring café had tried to make a play for Ninette. I had never seen anybody de-balled with a look before. Kanwaljit was never the same again. That's the look she had while kneading the dough that morning. And there was absolutely no doubt that that dough was me as she punched it with the force and strength of a mother protecting her child.

'One – you are much too old to have Francis as a close friend (wham!). He is just thirteen. You? You must be seventeen (wham!

wham!). Two – you don't go to play cricket every morning; you go somewhere else! And three (wham! wham! wham!) – instead of taking care of him, you are leading him astray! And I don't like it one bit (one final wham!).'

Should I tell her? Or shouldn't I? What was more important here? My word to Francis? Or self-preservation?

'Aunty, we play cricket. He is one of the best bowlers we have. But he is also interested in – '

'No, you don't, Raju!' hissed Francis in my ear, coming in with his kit and school bag. 'You promised you wouldn't ever tell anybody!'

'But these are your parents, Francis,' I hissed back. 'How much longer – '

'As long as it takes,' he replied, tossing his head. 'And you promised. Come on. We're getting late.'

'Why are you carrying your school bag?' Miriam asked suspiciously. 'Aren't you coming home after practice?'

'If I get late, I'll go straight to school – as I usually do. Come on, Raju!' he barked at me.

As we were leaving, Uncle Augustine stopped us.

'Now what?' said Francis, impatient to get out of there before his mother started on him again.

'Here, take some buns for your teammates. They might enjoy them.'

Before Miriam, who was turning a bright red and was ready to explode, could speak, we grabbed the buns and made a hasty exit.

Francis was sullen and silent as we walked to the nets.

I thought about the time, almost a year ago, when he had

barged into our shop in New Market and demanded an audience with my father. I'll never forget that day. He had a sheaf of paper in his hands with hundreds of doodles on them. They were all over the place, squiggly little drawings that didn't make any sense.

'What the hell are these?' I asked.

'You wouldn't understand,' he replied. 'But your father would.' He said this loudly enough for my father to hear.

My father, who was in his cabin, looked up from what he was doing, glowered at us, and then waved us in. We went inside, and very gently my father asked Francis what it was that he would understand.

When he spoke 'gently', you could bet that he wasn't too pleased. You must realize that even though he was my father, we never spoke to each other except at the breakfast table, when we went over the appointments scheduled for the day. And that was just a brusque exchange of words. 'Gently' was dangerous.

Francis, his head barely visible over my father's desk, banged his doodles down in front of my father. I flinched. He looked at Francis gravely. His fingers were rifling through the sheets. After glancing at them rather casually, he quickly sorted them into three bundles.

'The pile on the left are rings and earrings, at the centre – necklaces, and on the right are bangles and bracelets. Now tell me, where did you copy these designs from?'

Francis had that look on his face that umpires on the Calcutta maidan were terrified of, after an appeal he had made had been turned down. I pinched him hard. He controlled himself, took a deep breath, but you could see he was still annoyed.

'Mr Lalchand Uncle, I did not copy these designs! These designs are from my head.'

My father paused. Was that a hint of an expression I saw on his granite-like face? And if it was, what was he trying to express? His voice became even gentler.

'And you would like me to buy these designs from you?' he asked Francis.

'Ooof! Uncle Lalchand Sir! Why can't you understand?' Francis exploded.

No one spoke to my father like that. I flinched again. Was he angry? Disgusted with this young boy I had introduced to him? And therefore was he going to be pissed off with me? I mean *really* pissed off?

'I want you to learn me how to make these pieces,' he said, forgetting all grammar. 'I want to make these designs with my fingers.' He waved his fingers in the air. They reached somewhere just under my father's nose. 'My fingers are not meant to get dirty making shapes from maida!' Francis exclaimed in all seriousness. I didn't know whether to run out of the room or laugh nervously.

My father began to turn pink. If the pink turned to red, we were dead. Both of us. His body started quivering. He was about to lose his temper, and I had been at the receiving end of one of his tempers. Not nice. Not nice at all.

Except this time, he just burst out laughing. I was shocked. I had never seen him laugh. I never knew that he could laugh.

Finally, after taking a sip of water, he looked at the drawings again. 'How will you find the time? Cricket practice in the morning, school, homework, helping your father in the evening?'

'I won't play cricket.'

'Yes you will,' my father and I said in unison, perhaps agreeing about something for the first time in our lives.

'I know how important you are to the cricket team,' my father continued, 'so we must find a way. Raju, perhaps you can start the nets at six instead of seven?'

This was a side of my father I had never seen before. Concern for the cricket team, accommodating a friend of mine, not losing his temper, and actually laughing! What magic in Francis's drawings had brought about this transformation?

'I'll talk to your father and work something out.'

Francis, now really annoyed, with one of his famous 'hmphs' started gathering his designs.

'No, no, no. You can't tell daddy. Just the two of us.'

'But Raju knows,' said my father. 'That makes three of us.'

'Raju is my friend. I trust him with my life.'

At this my father looked at me, wondering what I had done to inspire such trust in one so young.

'Francis, your father is one of my oldest friends. If I don't tell him, don't you think I'll be betraying him in some way?'

'You old people don't know anything. All you think about is what might be 'good' for us. I think I want to *make* stuff. For my mother, my sister. Stuff that will make them happy. If you tell daddy, he'll be upset. He wants me to bake bread. He'll tell my mummy. Phuss! Finished. And she wants me to be a priest.'

What a tableau! A fat little boy, head barely above the table, about to shed tears of rage, nose to nose with my patrician-like father.

'Say promise,' insisted Francis clutching his drawings close to his chest.

My father blinked first.

'What will I get out of training you?'

'I don't know.' Francis looked very sullen. 'What do you want?'

'Now, *that* I don't know.'

Still nose to nose. If it wasn't so deadly serious, I'd have laughed.

'I know. Pick your favourite design from these drawings,' my father said.

Francis picked what looked like an elaborate necklace studded with emeralds, and handed it to my father.

'I promise I will never tell your father or anyone else about what you want to do, if you promise me that once my artisans have trained you, you will make this for my wife,' my father said solemnly.

'But that's my favourite design. I wanted that for my –'

'And now it's mine. Deal?'

'Okay,' said Francis as he reached out and shook my father's hand.

I have never seen Francis so excited. He was jumping up and down, a big grin on his face, shaking my father's hand vigorously.

'You surrendered rather easily?'

'Uncle Lalchand Sir, this one is for Raju's mum. I'll make a better one for my mother just you see.'

'The jeweller's son wants to be a cricketer. The baker's

son wants to be a jeweller. Who am I to argue with destiny? Raju will tell you where the workshop is. Be there by 7.30 every morning.'

For a year, every morning for an hour between net practice and school, and for an hour after school, Francis would go to my father's workshop and play with metals, and stones, and fire. I was terrified he would damage his fingers in some way. What would happen to our bowling attack? Francis just laughed at me.

But it was more than cricket that was worrying me. His evasive behaviour at home hadn't gone unnoticed and, if this morning's scene was anything to go by, things were going to come to a head soon.

They did.

A few evenings later, I walked from my shop to the D'Costa's to tell Francis that net practice was going to be a little late the next day.

There was a CLOSED sign on the glass door. The whole family was in there. Something was going on, something unpleasant. I hesitated. Should I enter the fray or come back later? Francis caught a glimpse of me and waved me in. I walked in.

Miriam took one look at me and took off. 'Here he is, the culprit. He is the one who has been a bad influence on Francis, encouraging him to do bad, bad things. First you tempted him to the cricket field, then you taught him how to lie, then you taught him to be stubborn, and now he has started stealing! Thanks to you my poor son will be going straight to hell!'

I was stunned by her assault. That was the only word I could think of. Assault. If she had a bread knife in her hands, which she often did, I'd have turned and run.

'Look!' she continued her rant. 'Look at all these pieces of jewellery,' she said, pointing to an array of trinkets lying on the counter.

To an eye like mine that was accustomed to jewellery, they were nothing but pieces of metal with bits of coloured glass. But they were beautiful designs and the uninitiated could mistake them for something valuable.

'He has been filching them from somewhere, and it's all because of your bad influence!'

I didn't know what to say. I had promised Francis never to divulge his secret. I looked at him. He nodded, giving me permission.

'Aunty Miriam, your son Francis is not a thief. He has not been filching these from anywhere. He has been making them in our workshop. Every day for two hours, sometimes on holidays, for the last one year, Francis has been learning how to become an artisan. Some of the designs that you see in our window display have been made by him. This one, for example, is the model for one of our bestselling items. He is not a thief; he is an artist.'

There was complete silence in the shop. Even the market went quiet, waiting as it were, for something momentous to happen.

Augustine looked at his son. *Is this my boy?* Half pride, half fear. Proud that his son had produced these; scared that he was going to lose his little boy to the jewellery business.

Miriam picked up a bracelet, almost reverently, slipped her wrist through it, and held her hand out to Francis waiting for him to tighten the clasp. She smothered an embarrassed

Francis in her ample bosom. Francis squirmed and struggled to free himself.

'Where did you get the idea that you could do this?' asked Augustine.

'From you,' Francis replied.

I don't understand,' a puzzled Augustine said. 'I bake bread.'

'Yeah. You bake the best bread in Calcutta. I want to make the best jewellery in the world.'

There was so much Augustine wanted to tell his boy, about how disappointed he was that Francis would never become a baker, how proud he was of his boy's skills as a designer, how much he loved his little boy. And he said it all in the only way he knew.

'Here. Have a Dutch Truffle.'

'Can I have a Nizam's kathi roll instead?'

I let myself out of the shop quietly, and into the normal raucousness of the market, secure in the knowledge that one more dream had come true.

A year after Francis died, so did Augustine. He never recovered from the shock of his son's death. Miriam and Ninette sold their home and the bakery, and moved back to Goa. They live in a small flat in Panjim.

I walked from St Thomas Church to the cemetery in Lower Circular Road where Augustine and Francis – artists both – lie side by side in two untended graves.

My wife wears the last design Francis ever made around her neck.

Just a trinket.

It looks real.

Homi

It used to be Dharmatala Street in the 1970s. It became Lenin Sarani later on and now that the Marxists have been ousted from power in Calcutta, it just might become Mamata Avenue. Who cares – Calcuttans or ex-Calcuttans still refer to it as Dharmatala Street.

My friend Homi lived there in a dilapidated but large sprawling house with his mother and her seven cats. He hated her and her cats intensely, in equal measure. This was in 1972. One corner of the house was blocked off from the rest, separate entrance and all – housing him, his grand piano, and his books. Homi got himself a dog. He did this because his mother hated dogs and he knew it would keep the cats away. All in all, it was a good idea. Or so he thought.

I was fairly indifferent to cats or dogs. I had this theory that anything with four legs deserved a fifth right up its arse. So I wasn't too happy when Homi phoned to say that I should meet him 'immediately, urgently' and at his place.

Homi's house was right next to Majestic Cinema. In the past, there might have been something majestic about the cinema and his house but, as it stood then, shops had taken over the pavement, posters advertising everything from prophylactics to pharmaceuticals crowded the walls, and neglected, crumbling pillars just about managed to keep it standing.

An aging lift, one of those floating cages with an even older liftman, took me up to Homi's.

'Listen to this,' Homi said, as he let me in.

No 'Hello.' No 'Nice to see you.' Social graces weren't Homi's forte. He walked up to his grand piano and began playing and singing.

I really hated my mother
And my mother she hated me
And most of the other women I knew
Tried to be mothers to me.
How I slept, what I drank, what I ate
Was more important you see
Than being a regular mate
They tried to be mothers to me.
So I went and bought me a dog
Life moves without a hitch
I could love him more than anyone else …
But he's such a son of a bitch.
So I avoid all things that are feminine
I'm as happy as I can be
So what! I say, if I never get laid
My dog's doing it for me.

'And the point of the song?' I asked, not daring to comment either on the lyrics or the tune.

'That's how we are going to open our play.'

'What play?'

'The one you're going to write, and I'm going to direct.'

'So I'm supposed to write a play about your life?'

'No. Not my life. Just … life.'

'That song is about you, Homi. It's the story of your life. And it's over. In a minute and a half of song. What's there to write about?'

'You're such a bitch!'

'Seriously, Homi, when did you last leave this room?'

He got up from the piano and started prowling around the room. He had a well-appointed study – a male room, dominated by the trophies he had won and pictures of women he had conquered or been conquered by. The women were very obviously older than him.

'Out there, in that world, all the women I know, and there are many, want to be my mother!' He paced up and down the room, looking at each of the pictures on his mantelpiece. '"Why?" – I cry out. Why?'

'So here's the first scene. I'm sitting at my piano. The lights come up, I sing my song, lights cross-fade to a dining table. My mother is waiting. I enter.'

Homi: Mum, I've told you not to wait up for me.

Ma: Yes, Homi darling, but I like waiting for you.

Homi: Have you eaten?

Ma: No.

Homi: Wives are supposed to wait for their husbands, if at all. Not for their sons. Where's Daddy?

Ma: Asleep.

Homi: Why didn't you eat and go to sleep too?

Ma: Somebody had to heat up the food for you. How can you eat cold food?

Homi: Mum, I'm thirty years old. If I want to, I can heat up my own food.

Ma: Boys are not supposed to do that.

'Sometimes, I wish mothers would prepare their sons for the world outside. Like most Indian males of my class, I have this love-hate relationship with my mother. Oedipal, Jungian, Freudian, or whatever. Not being very well read, I do not know how I should classify myself. So I don't bother. But all the girlfriends and wives I've had, turned out to be my "mother" or reasonable facsimiles thereof.'

'Come on, Homi, you're exaggerating. You were very happy when you were besotted with Divya.'

'Aaaargh, Divya!'

'She wasn't that bad!'

'She lived in this expensive apartment designed by the latest interior decorator in town. You could see the money on the walls, but little else. Me sitting morosely on the dining table. My cornflakes looking at me as if they might attack me. And me looking at Divya as if I might attack her.'

Divya: Homi, you need to be strong. Homi, eat your cornflakes. Homi, don't work late. Come back home early tonight. Working late isn't good for your health.

His rendering of Divya was perfect. A high-pitched, nasal, grating, fingernails-on-blackboard imitation. I couldn't help but laugh.

He grinned apologetically, 'That's not funny, you know. Not a month and a half of it. My mother and her cats were preferable. So I came home.'

'What about Aparna?'

'Aparna?'

And he launched into a whining take of Aparna.

Aparna: I've bought you some new shirts. You must dress well. Homi, I've stocked up your fridge. Make sure it's all finished before I visit again. Homi, I've got you new underwear.

'I had to chuck the food out of the fridge every time before she visited, never wore the shirts, and the underwear was too tight. She lasted three months. Three months! The price one pays for twice a week half-an-hour romps in bed.'

'Are you a male chauvinist or a misogynist? I can never tell with you.'

'If I'd known what was to follow, I'd have clung on to Aparna for dear life.'

He walked back to his piano, tickled the keys to play the song he'd composed, and then banged his fist on them. Something was troubling him.

'Want something to drink?' he said.

'Thought you'd never ask. Got any rum?'

'With water and ice, as usual?'

'That'll do fine.'

His hands shook as he poured the drinks. Something was really bothering him. He got some rum for me, and red wine for himself. By now the sun had set, and he went around the room switching on a few lamps, and finally settled down on a rocking chair. He looked gloomily at me.

'Remember Shishir? Came for three days, stayed for four months?'

'Don't I just! Made a pass at anything that moved, as long as it was male. I was worried about your mum's tom cats for a bit,' I smiled.

'He kept trying to clutch me to his rather hairy bosom.'

'Come. Come to mummy, darling Homio. I know how unhappy you are,' I said, still smiling and doing a fairly good imitation of Shishir.

'Of course I was unhappy. He'd come to stay for three days and it took me four months to get rid of him. And what a tearful farewell that was. I had to drag him down to a taxi while he kicked and screamed, threw him in it with his luggage, and paid the cab driver a thousand rupees to take him as far away as possible. Just because I'm a Parsi, and I play the piano, it doesn't mean I'm gay. Talk about stereotyping!'

'Tell me something. Is parsimonious a derivative of Parsi?'

'What?' He looked puzzled.

'So why haven't you poured me another drink?'

While he fixed me a drink, I thought about what he had said. His life might just make a good one-act play. If I could transport this room to a stage, it would be perfect. Autumnal colours. Pools of warm light. Shelves lined with books of all kinds – ancient mythology to Stephen Hawkins and everything in between. Hand-painted table lamps. Old Persian carpets strewn carelessly about the floor. I could see why he hated stepping out on to Dharmatala Street with its trams, buses, cars, rickshaws, handcarts, and into the human tide. People. People. People. You walked sideways on that street – there was so little space. Two-legged spiders scuttling across each other.

'And that's why I got myself a dog,' he said, handing me my drink. 'Man's best friend, or so I was told. We have a perfectly healthy relationship, even though he howls occasionally and tries to hump my knee. When denied the pleasure, he lunges for my jugular. I have the scars to prove it, and of course some trousers with permanent patches around the knees.'

'I wondered what possessed you – to get a dog! I don't know how you cope.'

'It keeps my mother and her cats away. And we have relaxed into a fairly normal routine now. He whimpers – I feed him. He barks – I take him to the loo. He howls – I kick him where it matters and let him out of the house. Go prowl, you lucky sod. He'll sniff around lampposts, drains, and hedges until he's tracked down his unsuspecting victim. Hours later he'll return, bedraggled, much the worse for wear, tongue lolling – a stupid beatific face that says it all.'

'Sounds familiar. Just like what you used to do.'

'Ha! Bloody ha! Very funny.'

We sipped our drinks for a few minutes in companionable silence. Faint sounds from the street floated in through the window. He'd opened a packet of salted cashew nuts. We munched. We sipped.

'Okay. I buy the premise. What next?' I asked.

'What are you talking about?'

'Your song. The play. You know …?'

'What about it?'

'The first scene. It's ready. We've established that you are a mother-hater, a misogynist, and a non-gay dog lover.'

'And then what?'

'And then we'll just have to work on something more. If this has to be about you, you're going to have to get out more often and live a bit.'

He looked at me, a bleak expression on his face. 'You've got to be kidding!'

I knew he'd hate that. 'Okay, okay. I'll work on it,' I said. 'We'll meet a month from now and see where the play's going.'

Many rums, wine, and cashew nuts later I staggered out on to Dharmatala Street. Not a soul. No trams. No people. The shops were shut. Perfect, I thought to myself. If Calcutta could be like this all day, it would be beautiful. You could actually see the building facades, remnants of the Raj, an odd decaying grace about them. Statesman House stood silently at the corner as newspapers were loaded on to trucks for dispatch. Opposite was the stately building of the Calcutta Electric Supply Corporation, lit up like a Christmas tree. A chai shop had just opened its shutters, so I ordered a cup and thought about the play. I mean, this was something I could really sink my teeth into. I knew exactly how I was going to structure it – bright, talented young man, fritters it all away, locks himself up in his room, and monologues himself to death. Black humour. Grim.

I slept through the day, and got up in the evening with a hangover. A hangover has no purpose other than to remind you that you should have behaved yourself the night before. It's just purposeless cruelty. It's like casual violence.

I had a shower, a cup of coffee, and began writing. For nearly a month I wrote. Relentlessly. Occasional early morning walks to the Victoria Memorial were the only times I stepped out of my room. Dustbins overflowed with yellow legal paper, a minor affectation of mine. This was before the PC, and I didn't know how to type. Fountain pens, empty. 'Don't Say Ink. Say Quink!' bottles littered the floor. I had rows of naaras strung across the room. Every time I finished a scene, I'd clip it to the naara. At the end of three weeks, I had fifteen scenes strung across my room. I started at one end of the room and read each page. As I walked from scene to scene, I felt more and more excited. I read the last lines.

Narrator: Homi's favourite mode of transport was the tram. 'It's electric, non-polluting, slow, and gentle,' he used to say. 'It's the last remnant of a gracious lifestyle.' So after he stepped out of his home, the first time in three years, it is ironic that he was run over by one. He would have liked that.

I took a bow. It was grim, dark and funny. It worked.

Now all it needed was some rewriting that Homi and I could do together; go into rehearsal and, in three months, have a Christmas opening. For the next couple of days, I worked on it a bit more and gave it to my father's secretary, Sandra, to type it up. Two days later, she handed them back. Perfectly typed except for some lines of dialogue that looked like this:

Homi: (livid) Listen you #$^#*. Get your @#$* out of my %&$(*)# house.

Sandra was a dear. She used some of the foulest language to describe most of my father's visitors. She knew the words, spoke them when needed, but couldn't type them. Certainly not for her boss's son. Oh no.

I landed at Homi's doorstep on the appointed day, at the appointed hour. Script in one hand, a bottle of wine that I could ill afford, in the other. It would be a good idea, I thought, to dull our critical senses before the first reading.

The door was closed. That was a surprise. He was the only resident on that floor and never shut his door. I rang the doorbell. A few minutes later, the door was opened by an old Parsi gentleman.

'Is Homi in?'

'No.'

'I have an appointment with him.'

'So you don't know.'

'What?'

'He was taking his dog to the vet. It slipped from the leash and ran across the road. Homi ran after it.'

'And?'

'The dog made it to the other side of the road. Homi didn't. He got run over by a garbage truck.'

Homi would have hated that!

Amol

Let me tell you a story I found both moving and humourous.

Amol was a Calcutta boy.

Through and through.

He was the son of Amulya Mazumdar, who had a small stall at the back of the New Market, the Corporation end of it, where he sold ribbons of every colour, buttons of every shape and size, clips, plastic or steel, combs, lace et cetera et cetera – everything a woman might need to make or repair anything she wanted. My friend Katy who had shifted to Bombay once told me, 'Bikash I can't get anything in Bombay because I don't know where to get it from. In Calcutta, if I need three feet of a quarter-inch broad ribbon, I know I'll get it at Amulya Babu's. But Bombay? I have to plan an expedition to get it.' Not surprisingly Katy and her family moved back to Calcutta not much later.

Of course I'd never met Amol in Calcutta but I did have a passing acquaintance with his father. I met Amol in New York, in the heart of Manhattan.

If you heard him speak for the first time as I did in New York, and if you closed your eyes, you'd be able to imagine him sitting on a 'rock' outside a paan shop, arguing the fate of the world with his college mates. Enquiring eyes smiled out at you through steel framed 'granny' glasses. His thick black hair was centre-parted, always pasted down to his rather large head, smelling faintly like Keo Karpin hair oil. 'In fact, it is jabakusum,' he proudly told me once we'd got to know each other and I'd become a regular at his establishment. 'Only one shop in Jackson Heights sells this.'

He spoke English with a broad 'Bangali' accent and, like all good Bengalis, he always remembered with great nostalgia *'the kul bridge blowing on Howrah Breeze.'*

Being a Calcutta person myself, we often swapped stories about the old city and exchanged memories of our younger days in the area around the New Market. His memories were very different from mine. After all, two decades separated us but some things had not changed. Nizam's was still there, behind the market and so was Nahoum's, right in the middle of it. How he had managed to reach this stationery shop in New York was anybody's guess. He refused to talk about it.

I did make the mistake of asking him once too often and he put me in my place. 'Bikash Babu,' he said 'do I *aks* you why you sit at home all day while your goodwife goes to work? No? Then why you are *aksing* me?'

Imagine, if you can, a small stationery shop owned by yes, you guessed it, an Indian from Gujarat. Of course, it had absolutely the best location on 1st Avenue at the corner of 54th Street, right in between Columbus' Bakery and a deli that sold freshly cooked specialty recipes from all around the world. Amol worked in this shop. In fact, he ran the shop. I'd never met the owner. Amol made everything available when you wanted it – that pencil sharpener late in the evening, that brand of coffee that only you drank, condoms of every shape, colour and size, staples and staplers, paper, both handmade and factory made. So far, there wasn't a thing that I required that he didn't have. And of course, *The New York Times*. You name it, he had it – even a bathroom mug – a must for every Indian who didn't feel comfortable with paper.

So it was refreshing to know that he wasn't doing it only for a living. He was (and he actually believed this) doing it because he felt that he was providing a much-needed service to the community. And all that even though he *didn't* own the shop. He just worked there. Always cheerful, always welcoming, always enquiring about how I was, how my wife was doing, and how the pollen was treating us that week.

If he didn't have something I needed, 'Come back in an hour,' he'd say, and I would see him charging out of his hole-in-the-wall establishment to source it from wherever he could.

So what's so special about that, I hear you ask. He was just doing his job, wasn't he?

When I use the term 'charging out', I use it rather loosely. Let's go back to the bathroom mug story. My mug had split near the handle, and was leaking. It is extremely difficult to conclude one's morning ablutions – as every self-respecting, bum-washing Indian will tell you, with a mug like that.

I walked into his shop.

'Aije Bikash Babu. Hwat I can gayt phor you thees hwanderful morning?' he asked in his broad Bengali accent.

I waited for the other customers to leave the shop, too embarrassed to tell him what I needed. Once I had him to myself, I asked him whether he had a bathroom mug.

'Ah! Paikhana'r mawg? That is why you were feeling shy in front of other customers?'

I explained that I'd been up and down First Avenue but couldn't find a place that sold one. Did he have one?

'No,' he said, 'but let me think for a moment. Okay. You mind the shop. I will be back in a jeefy.'

He left me in the shop and charged out. I followed him to the entrance and watched him. Two arms pumping, dodging people on the pavement, some of them stepping hastily out of his way as he pushed his wheelchair through them. All that to get me a mug.

Yes, he was on a wheelchair. He had no legs.

I had asked him once how that had happened, and he'd laughed and said, 'So many sad stories in the world, Bikash Babu. If people do not know of one more, there will be no harm.'

He came back triumphant, a few minutes later, this time at a more leisurely pace, with a smile on his face. I knew from that look that my morning problem had been resolved.

Now, I knew there were no plastic mugs available on First Avenue. Not anywhere.

'Where? … How?' I asked him.

He brandished the mug saying, 'Measuring jug. Same shape, same size. Only difference, it has measurements in ounces printed on the side. Will it do? That will be two dollars, thank you.'

They were the happiest two dollars I spent, and I congratulated him on his ingenuity.

'Legless, not brainless,' he said curtly and wheeled himself in to attend to a customer.

A few days later, I went in to pick up the Sunday papers. I saw him looking longingly at an ad for a pair of Gucci shoes. Remember that sentimental proverb about how bad one feels when one sees a man with no shoes until one sees a man with no feet?

He cut the ad out and pinned it on the board behind him.

'If you see any ads in the papers for shoes, cut them out for me,' he said. I told him that I would. I didn't have the heart to ask any questions.

The next day I gave him an ad for a pair of Nike shoes. He pinned it on the board. The third day, there was an ad for the world's first 'intelligent' shoes pinned next to my Nike ad. And the number of ads grew over the next fortnight. When I last looked at his board there must have been over sixty shoe ads pinned on it.

Some urgent work had cropped up in Calcutta. I had to head home for a bit. Amol gave me a whole lot of little gifts for his family in Calcutta. His father was thrilled when I walked into his shop and gave them to him. He was more thrilled hearing about Amol rather than with the gifts. In fact he didn't bother with opening the parcel. A few days later I discovered that there was one more parcel for him tucked away with my clothes. I walked to his shop to give it to him and there, under a sign saying 'freshly arrived from USA', were a whole lot of knick-knacks that I must have carried. Two months and many problems later, I returned to NYC.

I strolled into his shop to pick up the *New York Times* and was disappointed to see he wasn't there.

'Where's Amol?' I asked the man standing behind the counter.

'I *am* Amol. Bikash Babu, when did you come back?' he asked as he walked stiffly from behind the counter on his prosthetics, and shook my hand.

I was mortified at my blunder.

'Wait,' he said, 'I have something for you.'

He leaned back across the counter, took out a file from underneath it and handed it to me. It was full of ad clippings, the same ads we had started pinning on to his wall some months ago. I rifled through them. All of them were ads for shoes. There were shoes of every shape, colour, brand and design.

'Remember these?'

I nodded.

'I chose Gucci,' he said displaying his well-shod 'feet.'

'Blaady one month's salary, but waarth it,' he beamed at me.

I beamed back.

'This story you can tell. People need happy stories,' he said as he turned to greet the next customer that walked in.

Rathikanta

Only a handful of people in Calcutta had actually met and spoken to Rathikanta. The rest of the people who knew him or knew of him had only seen him sleeping.

It's what he did. Rathikanta slept. In buses, trams, tea shops, coffee houses – wherever he went, he slept. He slept through births, deaths, riots, battles, terror attacks, wars. He slept a lot.

He smiled lazily through sleep-laden eyes when told about the birth of his son. 'Why is everyone so surprised? What did they think? That I use my thing just for pissing?' He stretched himself out in the hospital waiting room, and promptly went back to sleep.

We were not surprised that he had become a father. We were surprised that he had managed to stay awake all through the child's conception. Little wonder then that he was known throughout Calcutta as 'Atiklanta Chatterjee.'

Atiklanta could best be translated as 'so weary.' He did have a world-weary air about him – one who had been there, done that, and seen it all. There was little he didn't know. And how he knew what he did, since he was never awake, was indeed a mystery.

In his younger days, he would go straight from school to his father's luggage and leather goods store, stick his nose into a book that he had scrounged off a friend, liberated from a library or bought from one of the many second-hand bookstalls in Free School Street and ignore any customer who walked in. They didn't exist for him. Until they showed an interest in the range of handmade suitcases which were stashed behind him in the shop. He would growl at them. Like a lioness protecting her cubs, he would have leaped out from behind his table and bitten them.

He had stored all his books in those suitcases.

'It seemed such a waste,' he once told me. 'All that volume of space lying around empty. It needed to be filled and I had nowhere to keep my books.'

Once, his father complained to my father that 'that feller Rathikanta will read anything you give him except his text books. Give him his physics book and within two minutes he is fast asleep in the middle of the shop.'

Rathi looked like a younger version of RK Laxman's Everyman, right down to his perfectly round glasses. He had begun balding early, in his twenties. Unlike Everyman he never wore a dhoti except to formal Bengali weddings and shraddhas at which, after the initial greetings or commiserations, he would attack the food with great gusto.

He ate with enthusiasm, relishing every loochi with alu dum, and ilish maach or chaatney. As one wag commented, 'He needs all that to give him the energy to sleep.' On principle, he never ate rice. 'Rice, you see, makes me very sleepy.'

On one such occasion, he overheard someone extolling the virtues of a holiday in Darjeeling. 'God help us from people who never talk about their holiday but "extol its virtues,"' he muttered to Beladi, his wife of many years.

But Darjeeling had caught his fancy.

On returning home that night, and after a short nap of course, out came volume 'D' of the encyclopedia. He got all the facts and figures about Darjeeling from there, and was rather unimpressed with the 'virtues' of the place until he chanced upon a Mark Twain quote: 'The one land that all men desire to see, and having seen once, by even a glimpse, would not give that glimpse for the shows of the rest of the world combined.'

Being a great fan of Mark Twain, a week later he was in Darjeeling. And three days into his 'tryst' with the 'Queen of the Himalayas' (his words exactly), Darjeeling decided to go on strike. This was perhaps for the first time in the history of Darjeeling that its citizens had gone on strike. No one quite remembers why they went on strike, but they did.

This didn't change his plans in any way since he wasn't your common or garden tourist. He didn't go on walks, or treks, and didn't get up early in the morning to watch the sunrise from Tiger Hill. He would find a comfortable place on a low wall somewhere, and nod off while watching the passers-by. No strike by disgruntled citizens had any effect on his chosen form of holidaying.

On the morning of the strike he'd gone to his usual perch, a wall that he had adopted, spread a shawl on it, and lain down on it with Bertrand Russell to keep him company. As he flipped through the pages idly, not really reading what Bertrand was trying to say, a group of desultory strikers were shouting their slogans of protest. It was their job to shout so they shouted. But he could see their hearts weren't in it.

Rathikanta, as was his wont, decided to take a nap. Which is what he did.

He got up rather suddenly, aware that the tone of the strikers had changed. There was a distinct enthusiasm in their sloganeering, a sort of energy which had been missing earlier. They had surrounded a jeep which had 'dared to come out on the roads during a strike.' The fact that it was a jeep on official duty didn't seem to matter. 'Arre bhai, our strike is against the gorment, and this is a gorment jeep. You might be on official duty, but it is our duty to make sure you don't do your duty.'

They chased the occupants of the jeep away, and began to debate on what they should do next. One of the more agitated strikers suggested they burn it. 'That's what they do in Calcutta when there's a strike.'

Having reached a consensus they attempted to do just that. Matchsticks were taken out, lighters were brought into use, a small bonfire was started on the backseat – but the jeep refused to burn.

Rathikanta was watching them from his perch. Amused. And mildly bored with their failed attempts. He yawned and started preparing himself for his next nap. One of the strikers noticed him.

'Who are you, sir? What you are doing here?'

'Oh, please ignore me. I'm here on a vacation.'

'From where you have come?'

'Calcutta.'

Immediately, a buzz went round. 'This tourist is from Calcutta. If anybody should know, it is him.'

Even though he pleaded ignorance, they were adamant that he give them some advice.

And thus began an idle conversation that led to an unexpected event.

'I can only tell you what I have seen,' he began absentmindedly. 'In Calcutta when they cannot burn public transport, they flip it on its head, and slash the tyres. As for burning, I cannot say because, frankly, I am afraid of fire.'

'But you must have seen how they do it?'

'Yes. Sometimes, when they flip it over, the petrol flows out. They wet a piece of cloth with it, set the cloth on fire, and throw it on the petrol.'

Having passed on his observations, and being rather bored with the conversation, Rathikanta decided to find another place to continue his nap, leaving the jeep to its fate and the strikers to their incompetence.

The next day, in Calcutta, we read about the twelve government vehicles that had been burnt in Darjeeling during the strike. And later in the day I got an urgent call from Rathikanta's wife, Beladi.

I rushed to the airport the next morning, caught a flight to Bagdogra in a Dakota of dubious airworthiness – with a goat on my lap (but that's yet another story) – took a long taxi ride which was as roadworthy as the Dakota was airworthy, and reached Darjeeling four hours later. I wondered, after the harrowing journey, why anyone would *want* to go to Darjeeling for a holiday. I picked Beladi up from the guest house and walked to the local jail to bail Rathikanta out. He had been arrested for aiding and abetting riots and disturbing the peace under Section god-knows-what of the IPC.

At the police station we found Rathikanta in the corner of a cell full of protestors, with a copy of Kierkegaard's *Edifying*

Discourses in Diverse Spirits lying across his chest. He was, of course, fast asleep. I think Bertrand Russell might have been more comfortable in jail than Kierkegaard.

A bit of charm, a touch of corruption, and many explanations later, we managed to get Rathikanta out. He insisted that since I was already in Darjeeling, I should stay on and do some sightseeing.

'Rathi, we can't stay here,' Beladi said. 'You have been let off, and we have to leave the hill station precincts within forty-eight hours.'

'Tch! Forty-eight hours is a long time. And Bikash has come all the way to rescue us, we should give him a good time. Tomorrow morning – sunrise from Tiger Hill. How about it?'

This I had to see! No, not the sunrise from Tiger Hill … but Atiklanta! Awake! At four in the morning? This was going to be one for the history books. So I agreed.

'In the meantime, let's walk to Keventer's for some sandwiches and tea. Such a pleasant afternoon, isn't it?' he said.

We ambled up the hill to Keventer's. Nowadays, I believe it has become a fast-food place. But that is just hearsay. I wouldn't know for sure but I could believe it. In those days, it was a genteel little place that sold thinly sliced cucumber sandwiches with some fine Darjeeling muscatel tea as an accompaniment.

We reached Keventer's, a five-minute walk away about half an hour later since, on the way, a number of people – total strangers – stopped us and spoke to Rathi as they would to an old friend. They invited him to their homes and offered him presents. I think one of them even offered his daughter's hand in marriage, much to Beladi's amusement.

This sleepy-head 'Atiklanta' had become, overnight, 'Bahadur Singh' to the locals.

We settled down at a table near the door and Rathi ordered for the three of us. He sniffed the air around us, looked accusingly at me and asked, 'Bikash, why are you smelling of goats?'

In my haughtiest manner I told Rathi and Beladi, 'The plane I came by was part cargo, part passenger. And one of my co-passengers in the cargo hold at the rear of the plane was a goat. When we hit an air pocket, it landed on my lap and refused to leave until we landed. It is the price one pays to rescue one's disruptive, disreputable friends from the clutches of the law.' I needn't have bothered with the haughtiness. They were killing themselves laughing, trying to imagine what I looked like with a goat in my lap. Fortunately it was a baby goat.

In the meantime, Keventer's had been cleared by the owners. All the other tourists were asked to leave. We were the only customers left. One by one the locals, who didn't usually patronize the place, walked in and silently occupied the seats around us. One of them who didn't come in, but stood at the entrance, I recognized as a policeman from the thana from where we had rescued Rathi. He was now in plain clothes, and was there, obviously, to keep an eye on us. He accosted everyone who came in and then made some hurried notes in a dirty, dog-eared diary.

Rathi recognized him too. He got up, went to the door, and tapped the fellow on the shoulder. 'It's mighty cold out here.

Why don't you come in and make your notes? Have a cup of tea with us.'

The policeman scurried away, as though he might contract some imagined form of contamination or disease from contact with us. As Rathi resumed his seat he was greeted with a round of raucous applause. Word would spread within the next hour that not only had he 'escaped' from jail, he had accosted a policeman and had made the policeman flee. Bahadur Singh was a true bahadur, indeed!

It became distinctly uncomfortable by the time our tea and sandwiches had arrived. Not one of the customers said a word. They just looked at Rathi as if a saviour had descended in their midst. And we munched our cucumber sandwiches and sipped our tea in silence.

'Let's plan tomorrow morning's trek to Tiger Hill,' Beladi said, turning to Rathi. But of course she got no response. He had, as usual, fallen into a deep slumber.

When Beladi and I tried to talk to each other, we were 'shushed' by the rest of the patrons. 'Let Bahadur Singh sleep.' A hero needed his sleep.

We decided to walk down Mall Road and tip-toed our way out of there. In those days a mall wasn't a supermarket, it was the heart of the town. No cars were allowed in this mall and one could amble across it, catching some fantastic views of the Himalayas.

We stopped at the chowrasta and caught a glimpse of the Kanchenjunga in all its evening splendour. Fortunately for us it was a crisp, clear day and the view was magnificent. The temperature dropped rather suddenly, so we walked back to Keventer's at a brisk pace to discover that Rathikanta was still asleep, still surrounded by his fans. Only now he had sprouted a balaclava (monkey cap to the rest of us) around his head, and was wrapped in a multi-coloured blanket that would have done Jacob's son Joseph proud.

Since we had to wake up early in the morning to go to Tiger Hill, we apologized profusely to the rest of his fans, and woke Rathi up and returned to our lodge.

I didn't get to see the sunrise on Everest from Tiger Hill. Or Rathi awake at that hour.

At the lodge, waiting for us, were three police jeeps with our various pieces of luggage packed into them.

'I thought we had at least forty-eight hours,' Rathi protested.

'Things change, Mr Bahadur Singh,' the OC said sarcastically.

Without much explanation we were driven through the night to Bagdogra and, after a long wait there, surrounded by the police who, it has got to be said, did ply us with cups of hot, sweet tea we were escorted on to the same plane in which I had arrived the previous afternoon.

We strapped ourselves in and, before Rathi went off into yet another nap, he muttered, 'Bela, remind me to donate my collection of Mark Twain to the local library. I never want to visit *him* again.'

We flew back to Calcutta, accompanied by the gentle snores of Atiklanta and the occasional bleating of a goat.

Gopa

Lindsay Street runs right across the front of the New Market. In my childhood I always thought the street had been named after the Lindsay Dyeing and Dry Cleaning Company that stood at the end of Chowringhee Road. That it was the other way round, I discovered much later. When I had told Dada Prita who owned the dry cleaning shop about my theory behind the history of the name, he had a good laugh and set me right.

The funny thing about Lindsay Street was its parking lot. It was in the centre of the road and the traffic moved around it. Rumour has it that this was from the days of the ghora garries or horse carriages. They didn't want the horses too close to the entrance of the Market for too long. After all, one wouldn't want the memsaabs stepping into horse shit as they elegantly stepped off the garries. This, in all likelihood, is true, as tucked away between the parked cars at fairly regular intervals, are some old structures that look like horse troughs.

It is early morning. No traffic moves on Lindsay Street and, as the market clock strikes four, the first stirrings begin – a milkman with two ten-gallon cans slung over either side of the back seat of his cycle rides slowly towards Free School Street; a man with four wire baskets filled with eggs rushes to make his deliveries; a third man wraps his sacred thread lazily around his ear as he picks up his lota and ambles into a little lane to perform his morning ablutions.

Slowly the street comes alive.

This street seemed wider in the old days, with horse-drawn carriages clip clopping through at a leisurely pace, rickshaws with the not-so-well-off memsaabs being pulled along. The average speed was ten miles per hour.

Today, with all the fast cars, the crowds and the mushrooming of pavement shops, the average speed is five miles per hour. That is progress.

Today the New Market moves along at a far more hectic pace. Old shopkeepers have given way to new ones, and old shops selling exotic goods from all over the world have given way to cheap, shoddy products that we rush to buy from rude salesmen. That too, is progress, I suppose.

However, there were some shops that had remained untouched by time.

In Hertford Lane, opposite the clock tower – the lane that joins Lindsay Street to Sudder Street, a roadside vendor has already set up shop. His modus operandi hasn't changed for at least two generations. Jalebis still turn to a rich gold in a huge kadai of boiling oil. Next to it is a large tray of uncooked samosas waiting in military formation to be deep-fried. On a small fire next to the kadai, a dirty black aluminium dekchi full of a milky concoction that once upon a time could have been called tea, still boils as the market clock strikes five. A young lad pours out two glasses of the boiling liquid into moderately clean glasses, and hands them to us – Dada Prita the dry cleaning man, and me.

Prita had just got back from his morning walk. Yes, morning walks happened really early in Calcutta, and I was waiting for my truckful of flowers to arrive from my bagan bari. We took each other's presence for granted. This was a daily ritual both of us enjoyed. No words were exchanged until we'd blown air over the steaming tea in great anticipation and taken our first few sips.

'How is everything going?' I asked him.

Over the years, Prita Babu had kept a fairly detailed diary about the happenings in New Market. I envied him his storytelling skills and occasionally, on a morning, as on this morning, he had a spring in his step which was far removed from his post-morning walk crawl. This was a sure sign that he had heard a new story and had finished writing it.

'Everything is marvellous,' replied Dada Prita.

'That I can see,' I said. 'So am I going to hear it today or are you going to keep me in suspended suspense?' I asked, forgetting my grammar in my excitement.

'Am I that obvious?'

'Indeed you are,' I said and we both smiled. He didn't take any offence. None was intended. We both knew that.

'Have you heard about Gopa's latest adventure?'

'Ganguly Gainjeewala's daughter? Ki holo? What happened?'

If you liked Ganguly Babu, you called him Ganguly Gainjeewala, as I did. If you didn't, you called him Binod Brawala. As you might have inferred, he had a shop that sold undergarments for men and women.

'A few days before, Gopa had been at loggerheads with her family, as she usually is,' Prita began.

We all knew Gopa. She was a 'marketeyr bachcha' as all the children of all the shop owners were known. She was known for her vocal skills and sang with great gusto at all the New Market functions. The family was an uncomplicated middle class family. Her elder brother was Jojo, her younger Rono, and she was trapped in the middle, and had all the complexes that come with being a middle child. Add to that the fact that she was a daughter, and you can see why any problems she had were only compounded. Their mother, a seemingly gentle lady, ruled the house with an iron fist. No one dared argue with her. Mr Ganguly, the mild-mannered patriarch, was the one who handled the family's woes with tact and humour.

'Oof Prita Babu! Gopa is always at loggerheads with somebody or the other. One day it will be with the Corporation, the next with the University. What did her bechara family do?'

Prita began the tale.

'Baba,' Gopa said innocently that morning at the breakfast table, 'you deal in women's underwear and yet you haven't employed a single woman in your shop?'

Her mother, who could read and assess her family's mood, knew trouble was brewing. She could sense it. She hoped Gopa's father would ignore the question.

'Don't say a thing,' she instructed him.

Too late.

'What would be the point?' he answered Gopa absent-mindedly.

Normally, he would have deflected the question. But this morning he was distracted by something he had read in the papers. Ajoy Mukherjee's United Front government had fallen and another election had been announced. This was going to have an unpleasant effect on things in Calcutta and New Market in particular.

His wife groaned.

'Ki holo?' he asked his wife.

'Don't you think women would find it more comfortable dealing with women in a shop selling women's underwear?' Gopa continued.

'No bhadramahila has complained as yet, so one can safely assume most women are comfortable dealing with the salesmen in my shop, by and large,' he said, completely forgetting that this was Gopa he was getting into a discussion with.

'Most women who come by are often rather large,' Jojo said with a wry smile.

'Jojo, put your mouth to better use. Eat with it instead of making stupid observations,' Mrs Ganguly said quietly but firmly. 'And if you know what's good for you, you'll stay out of it.'

She knew both her husband and daughter well, and knew that another episode of Gopa vs Father had begun.

'Another episode?' I inquired.

'Remember the tokriwallah's andolan?' Prita asked me.

'Eeeesh baba! Don't I just? Ki kando!'

'Who do you think was behind the "kando"?'

I was surprised. 'Gopa?'

About three months earlier, Gopa had started a seemingly innocent conversation about the tokriwallahs of the market. Tokriwallahs were a loose-knit federation of porters who carried your shopping for you in their handmade tokris, followed you around from shop to shop and delivered all your shopping to your car, taxi, rickshaw or whatever mode of transport you were planning to take. All this for a pittance. And for a bit of plus to the pittance, if you lived within a mile or so from the market, they'd even deliver your shopping to your doorstep. It was a service unique to New Market and still exists.

'Baba, don't you think the tokriwallahs should charge per tokri as opposed to per piece of shopping?'

Five minutes later there was an all-out argument at the breakfast table and two days later they were on a strike instigated, perhaps 'inspired' would be a better word, by Gopa.

The end result of that little exercise was a disgruntled bunch of shopkeepers who contributed a rupee per purchase to the tokris and the shoppers who had to fork out five rupees more per tokri. The most disgruntled, however, were the tokriwallahs. They had lost revenue during the strike, which they hadn't yet recovered, and of course they regretted the loss of goodwill.

As a result, Gopa wasn't very popular with anybody, not even the tokriwallahs.

'Aachha Prita Babu, please explain something,' I said. 'Both you and I have shops in this area. Yet, I do not know anything about the people here and you know everything. How is that?'

'Arre, Bose Babu, not everyone buys flowers. But everyone has dirty clothes. So they come to my shop regularly and talk. And I listen.'

'Aijay Hari, aaro doo-to cha de, aar doo-to shingara,' he gestured to the teashop boy.

Once the round of tea and piping hot samosas had been served, I looked expectantly at Prita. He bit into his samosa leisurely and took a satisfying sip.

'Ah! Bolun bolun! What did Ganguly Gainjeewala's Gopa do?' I asked impatiently.

'Bose babu, you really enjoy a good gossip, no?' said Prita playfully.

'Na na, ki bolchhen moshai,' I replied sheepishly. 'I just like the way you weave a tale but you do take your time going about it,' I complained.

'So the argument continued at the Ganguly home,' Prita picked up from where he had left the story.

'Most women are too embarrassed to complain about salesmen, Baba,' Gopa maintained.

'But why should they complain? What on earth are you talking about? What do they have to complain about?'

Mr Ganguly was truly perplexed. He had been working in the shop since he was fifteen, under the eagle eye of his father. He had seen women come and go all his life. Not one of them had been remotely coy about asking for underwear of any kind. They knew the brand they wanted and the size. They stated their needs, collected their parcels, paid the price and walked out. They even exchanged a pleasantry or two with him on the way out.

'Women customers need saleswomen, not men,' Gopa insisted.

'I thought you wanted equality for women.'

'Exactly. You have salesmen for your male customers. You should get saleswomen for your women customers.'

'True equality means women shouldn't mind whether there are men or women behind the counter.'

'Baba, you do not know the meaning of equality. You've always treated Ma and me as second class citizens.'

At this, Ganguly Babu lost it. But before he could say anything, his wife stepped in.

Very sternly she said, 'Ai Gopa, chhoto mukhay boro katha. That is disrespectful. And I'm quite capable of fighting my own battles, thank you. You can shut up and leave the table.'

Gopa left with a parting shot. 'No wonder women all over the world are burning their bras in protest.'

'Good for my business,' her father shouted right back.

Others joined the battle. It was going to be an interesting time not just in the Ganguly household and their shop, but in the New Market too.

At three that afternoon, Gopa fired the first salvo.

A group of over a hundred college girls dropped into the shop at the same time, with ads of foreign bras, and demanded they be shown the bras advertised. The girls were brazen with their demands, and the salesmen – mild-mannered aging Bengali gentlemen – were rather horrified at some of the skimpy clothes the girls had on.

Work came to a halt. Genuine customers couldn't get into the shop. Slowly but surely over the next half hour, the area outside the shop started overflowing with people – protesting students and genuine customers alike.

From somewhere a guitar appeared, as did Gopa. The guitar was passed to her and she started singing *Ekla Chalo Re*. Across a sea of protesting heads her eyes locked with her father's. Her crystal clear voice carried through to him. His face said it all. He didn't know whether to be angry with her, or proud that she had such a lovely voice. He smiled.

Gopa 1 – Father 0

The next morning when Gopa got out of bed, she found herself knee-deep in water. Her room had been flooded the night before by a tap that she had probably left turned on when there was no water supply. She didn't normally make this sort of mistake. It was while she was mopping up her room that she heard her father approach, singing. He too had a crystal clear voice. In fact there was little doubt that she had inherited her talent from him.

He came and stood in the doorway, watching her mopping up. He started singing her favourite Bhatiyali. He had a wide grin on his face as he sang.

Bondhu okuley bhashaya bondhu re koi roila re bondhu koi roila re
Oh dear friend, where have you gone, setting me afloat in the shoreless sea?

In the past her father had admonished her for being careless and had helped her mop her room. Today, however, he was just enjoying her discomfiture. She knew she would receive no help from him and that she was alone 'in the shoreless sea.'

He had drawn level. Gopa 1 – Father 1.

The following week, things got worse. Gopa would be in a procession one moment protesting against the escalation of the Vietnam War in front of the United States Information Service building (it was a short walk from the market), and the next she'd be at the market leading the escalation of the war against her father.

But every move Gopa made was countered brilliantly by her father.

The score sheet soon read Gopa 5 – Father 5

Mrs Ganguly decided to call a halt to the battle. Strained silences at home, sudden temper tantrums, Jojo and Rono taking full advantage of the situation and bunking college to keep an eye on things – the matter was becoming unmanageable. At dinner one night, she made the announcement. 'The war is over. I am calling it an honourable draw and the two of you are calling a truce.'

'Only if Baba employs a woman,' said Gopa resolutely.

They all looked at him expectantly. Much to everyone's surprise, he agreed. 'But on one condition,' he said. 'Since a saleswoman was your idea, I think you should be the first woman to stand behind the counter.'

Gopa, always a good sport, agreed. 'I will start on Monday,' she said.

On Monday, Gopa reported to work at eleven. By eleven-fifteen, she'd committed her first faux pas.

A lady in her mid-thirties walked into the shop, saw Gopa and smiled.

'How can I help you, mashima?' Gopa asked.

The smile disappeared. Instantly.

'Last bheek I was chhotdi. This bheek I'm mashima? You must get a betaar quality salesgirl, Mr Ganguly. This girl is a nonsense,' she said as she sailed out of the shop.

'Gopa. I suggest you sit at the cash counter for a while. Watch and learn,' her father told her.

Gopa watched. And Gopa learnt. That gender didn't matter.

'Where is Narain Babu?' a fortyish-looking lady walked into the shop.

'Arre Rama Boudi,' Narain greeted her, appearing from the backroom. 'How is Bachchu? Any better?'

'A little ambal, that's all. He had churan from the ting-ting man at school. Ambal to hobeyi!'

'Aar Amalda. How is he?'

'He has got a promotion,' Rama said proudly. 'He's sent some mishti for all of you. Here it is,' she said handing over the box of sandesh.

'And here is your parcel,' said Narain handing over three Maidenform bras.

She took her boxes, paid the money and left. She never stated her needs. She didn't need to. She was an old customer and Narain Babu not only knew her requirements but, over a period of time – a remark here, a complaint there, a worry mentioned – was familiar with her family too.

'Where is Keshto Kaka?' a young twenty-two-year-old bounced into the shop.

'Boonu! Bhalo aachho?' said Keshtoda, a toothless old man of sixty or so. 'What a surprise. You've come today?'

'Yes. I was free. How is Mita? How are her English lessons?'

'Fluently bhool bhal bolchhe. But arre baba! Ki accent. Theek Rex Harrison in *My Fair Lady*.'

'What is this, Keshto Kaka? Why have you given me 36B? You know it's A.'

'That was last year Ma! Take my word, it is B now.'

'Okay. If you say so. Tell Mita to call me. I want to check on her spoken English,' she said, paying Gopa at the cash counter.

Many customers came and went in the course of the day. Each had a special salesman. Each had over the years developed a special relationship which went way beyond the common, mundane business of buying and selling.

A day sitting behind the counter and observing what was happening was, as Gopa put it later, an equivalent to getting a Bachelor's degree in sales and a Master's in life.

Later that night at the bus stop, on their way home, Gopa and her father waited for the number five to Shyambazar. The buses were running a bit slow that day. Actually they ran slow pretty much every day, but that day perhaps because of the tension between father and daughter they seemed to be running a bit slower than usual.

'Want some jhaal moori?' Gopa's father asked her.

'I could have some,' she replied.

Ganguly told the mooriwalla to make two packets with lots of jhaal.

'Well,' Ganguly Babu said, 'did you enjoy your first day at work?'

'It was quite the eye opener and I had a splendid time,' she said. 'But I think it was also my last day at work,' she added ruefully. 'And I promise never to harass you again about the way you run your shop.'

'That would be extremely unfair,' her father said, smiling gently, 'Life would be very boring if you didn't.'

They waited for their bus, at peace with each other and with the world, munching their moch mochay moori.

I burst out laughing when Prita finished his tale. 'I did not know that Ganguly Gainjeewala had a sense of humour.'

We paid Hari and walked on to Lindsay Street. It was a handsome street. The New Market stood majestically on one side, and on the other a row of grand old mansions that had seen many andolans in the past and, with Gopa in the vicinity, would see many more in the future

The flowers I had been waiting for from my bagan bari had arrived in a van: chrysanthemums, roses, dahlias, gladioli and deep maroon carnations. I took a handful of flowers, and handed them to Prita Babu as the market clock struck the half hour past five. 'Here, Prita Babu. The first carnations of this winter. For Bhabhiji. See you tomorrow.'

Prita Babu nodded his thanks and I watched him walk away with the small bouquet of flowers in one hand, and a faraway look in his eye. He had perhaps already started plotting his next story.

Mita

We broke off rather elegantly, I thought.

She said, 'This relationship is going nowhere,' while nibbling at a chingdi maacher kabiraji cutlet in a little Bengali restaurant off Elgin Road.

I said, 'Bitch!' as I finished off the last of the kethor jhol.

So off she went and married my best friend.

Now, if your ex-girlfriend decides to get married to your ex-best friend, and after the heartbreak and the recriminations are over, you should remember to take back the house keys and change the locks.

When I staggered home one night, I found Mita curled up in my bed, nine years after she had left me for that back-stabbing bastard, and I knew right then, in my semi-drunken state, that this might not be a good thing.

She was in a restless sleep, the sheets tangled around her in disarray, one delectable leg sticking out, streaks of mascara trailed down her cheeks. She had obviously been crying. A half-consumed bottle of my favourite single malt lay on the bedside table; there was no glass. This must be serious, I thought to myself, if she was guzzling straight from the bottle.

In the old days, she liked it when I woke her up if I came in late and, if I didn't, she would ask me accusingly the next morning why I hadn't.

I stood there and watched her sleep.

I'd had plans for us. Mita was going to be my way out of the New Market life. Or so I had thought. It was not much fun being Hotchand Motiram's son – selling fancy watches and clocks for a living. She was my classmate in Jadavpur and had all the finesse and sophistication of a tea garden owner's daughter. She taught me to appreciate music, art and above all theatre – to which I am still passionately addicted.

But it didn't work out that way.

She ran away with my best friend and married him.

Nine years, one bastard husband and two children later, here she was and she could still turn me on – so now would not be a good time to wake her up. I backed away, went out to the living room and crashed on the sofa.

My nostrils twitched. Fresh coffee. I opened my eyes. Mita was sitting opposite me, freshly showered, in one of my shirts and little else, looking disapprovingly at me, pouring out what smelt like my Colombian roast.

'Why didn't you wake me up when you came in?' she asked accusingly.

Nothing changes. Yet, everything had, her troubled, wary, near-panic eyes told me.

'It's going to have to wait,' I said.

'What is?'

'Whatever it is you want to talk about. I have a Skype conference call coming in and I have to concentrate on it. Whatever it is, it's going to have to wait. I can't have your problems cluttering my concentration.'

'But it's important.'

'So is my con-call. Mita, you haven't spoken to me in nine years; what's a couple of hours more?'

I had over the nine years managed to move away from New Market. But I was still dealing in timepieces, as Mita pointed out later. Antique ones from every corner of the earth, but still they were just watches. The family business continued, much to her amusement.

She didn't speak for the next two hours, while I argued and negotiated with my colleagues and clients across the seas. Though she didn't say a thing, she would occasionally stroll across my line of vision to the kitchen for a cup of coffee, or bring a glass of juice for me, and those long legs I had often climbed up, inch by inch ... I didn't remember a word of the Skype conference call.

I switched my Mac off, and angled it so that I could see her reflection on its dark screen. She was looking out of the window. I couldn't quite see her expression, but she was just as beautiful as she had been nine years ago when she walked out on me. She sensed she was being watched, turned and looked at me.

'Time to talk?' she asked me.

'I'm starving. Let's go out and talk over lunch.'

'I would much prefer staying in.'

'And I would like to go somewhere so that you are forced to put more clothes on,' I muttered.

She slipped on one of my long kurtas and knotted one of my soft belts around her waist. 'Will this do?'

My kurta had never looked better.

Half an hour later we were ensconced in one of the family cabins in a small restaurant behind New Market. It was a perfect wintry day for kebabs and biryani, and this place was famous for just that. It was also famous for the holes drilled into the wooden cabin walls so that peeping Toms could sneak a peek at snogging couples. Since there was little danger of that happening, I didn't order some soft roti ka aata to plug the holes before we settled down.

This was not the kind of place where you ordered food course by course. You just ordered the lot together, and soon our table was covered with kebabs of various meats and lots of raw onions. They would be a deterrent to any postprandial billing and cooing – and I wasn't taking any chances.

Mita picked up a sheekh and just before biting into it, said rather nonchalantly, 'My husband is having an affair and I don't know what to do about it.'

I went cold. So did the uneaten kebabs. Was I imagining it or had the restaurant beyond our cabin fallen silent? Why was she telling me this? We hadn't exchanged a word in the longest time. Did she want to make a comeback into my life? After nine years? Did I want it? I was pretty sure I didn't. It had taken me some time to get over her. While packing, she had made a flippant remark about me – that I was good for 'cock and conversation' but she was looking for something deeper. That had hurt. I had come to terms with living alone.

She just sat there. Tears flowed down in copious amounts.

Damn! I thought. She's in a mess and all I can think about is myself.

There was only one way to handle this. A boat ride on the river was called for.

We left the food uneaten, settled the bill and hopped into a cab. On the way, I picked up a bottle of Old Monk at a booze shop. Fifteen minutes later we were being rowed down the

Hooghly by Abdul, a weather-beaten ancient mariner – grey hair, grey beard, and an ebony body that had seen better days – in a boat that had never seen a good day in its entire life. It had been creaky and leaky when I first bought a ride a decade and a half ago. It still was.

But I knew it and Abdul well. In times of crisis they had often come to my rescue. And I could sense that this was going to be a major one.

The dam burst. She bawled, loud and long. Abdul, who I was sure had witnessed many such scenes before, continued rowing without a glance in our direction.

It took a while, but she exhausted her tears. I handed her my handkerchief. She wiped her eyes, blew her nose and smiled wanly at me. I passed the Old Monk to her and she choked on it.

'What is this?' she exclaimed. She took the bottle out of its brown paper wrapping. 'Ah, the much-needed ministrations of the monk!'

'Got used to the good stuff, have you?'

'No. This is still the best. I'd just forgotten,' she said, taking another swig.

'Feeling better?'

'U-huh,' she grunted. Which could mean anything.

She dipped both her hands in the river, scooped up a handful of water and rinsed her face. She was like that. No hesitation, no worries. Was the water clean? Was it hygienic? Nope. Just a scoop and wash. She looked better than I'd ever seen her look.

'How could he … she do this to me? To us?'

I didn't reply.

'Well?'

'Oh, were you expecting a reply? I thought the question was purely rhetorical.'

'But how could they?'

'Who is she?'

'Someone I knew very well, or I thought I did.'

I couldn't resist it. 'Ironic isn't it? Someone I knew very well walked off with you.'

'Yeah,' she said, sounding wry and bitter. 'I remember your favourite line: "Consequences. They come and bite you in the arse in this life."'

We shared another swig.

'Mita, I don't want to know the hows and the whys. What I do want to know is what you're going to do about it.'

But she wasn't listening.

'I should have guessed some time ago when he started getting compulsive about neatness and discipline at home. Hell, kids make a mess – a toy here, a crayon there, but no. He'd stand over them like a maniacal Mary Poppins and get them to clean, clean, clean.'

'Seeing too much of your mother, was he?'

'See, you got it. How come I didn't?'

I stared at her, uncomprehending.

'She did stay with us for ten thousand and eighty minutes. And each minute felt like a day,' I said.

They were the longest seven days of my life – when her mother had stayed with us. I didn't interfere with her day-to-day fussiness about the right place for the right things, but the last straw was when I opened my cupboard and found my clothes marked Monday, Tuesday, Wednesday … She had to go.

'In all the years I was with you and then with Ajay, I noticed that men always … why do men always have a post-coital look that borders on the triumphant?'

'Do we? I've always thought of it more as an expression of relief. A sort of phew-that-went-off-well look.'

'He'd go shopping and come back with that look. He'd run out to do some chores, come back late from work, say he was out with the boys … and every bloody time he'd come back with that look, you know.'

She talked about a lot of incidents that on the one hand were frightening – her husband's sudden tendency to bully the kids and her, his attempt at violence which she quelled instantly with a kick in his groin; and some other instances that were quite hilarious – accompanying her when she went lingerie shopping and his insistence on watching her try her 'knickers' on in the changing room. 'Knickers' was the word he used, she pointed out.

'But it just seemed too far-fetched. I'd be sitting out in mum and dad's garden with the kids, he'd go in to help mum, and a few minutes later he'd return wearing that look. Maybe, I thought, I'm imagining the look. After all, the only other woman in the house was my mother.'

A boatman going in the other direction called out to Abdul. He replied and I smiled.

'You're not taking my predicament seriously,' Mita complained, piqued.

'The boatman there asked Abdul if he'd caught any fish today. "Two big ones," Abdul replied and looked at us. That's why I smiled.'

'On one of our many visits, and they were happening very often, I needed some documents of mine from her cupboard. They weren't in their usual place so I opened another drawer and there in that drawer was an identical pair of "knickers" he had watched me try on and buy.'

'Your kind of lingerie?'

'No. I think his idea was that I should wear *her* kind of lingerie. "Knickers" was her word, I remembered.'

I stared at her, dumbfounded.

'You know what she told me when I confronted her? She said she didn't owe me any explanation, because she was my mother. "You married an idiot," she said. "He was available, so I took him. I don't have to help you understand why I am the way I am. But if you are like me, as you say, though I rather doubt it, and if you have in you even one-tenth of the contempt I have for the world, you might make something of your life." And then she smiled. She looked like a well-fed lizard with a moth in its mouth.'

She did a more than passable imitation of her mother and I couldn't stop myself from laughing.

'It's not funny, you know.'

'No, not at all. It's just the way you're telling it,' I said, only just stopping myself from breaking out into another round of laughter.

'I could go on,' she said after a pause.

'No, please. Later. Then you can tell me all the gory details,' I said. 'I don't think I can take any more now. Ajay and your mother sound like something out of an Iris Murdoch story.'

'How could she do this to me? And that wimp! How could he?'

The tide had changed. Abdul began turning the boat around very gently. She reached out for the bottle and took another swig.

'What am I going to do?' she wailed.

'Mita, it's not about you any more, not just you anyway. It's about your children, your father, your siblings. If this comes out in the open, your family and all its extensions are going to be ripped apart.'

'I need to get a job, a place of my own, my children. Where will we stay? How will I take care of them?'

'The guest suite on the third floor is yours. Needs to be cleaned a bit, but it is there – for the moment. You can get a place of your own later.'

We rode back to the Chandpal Ghat in silence.

She had a bleak look about her, contemplating a not very pleasant future. I had a silly grin on my face, which of course she misinterpreted.

'Hey. About you and me. We aren't getting back together, that's a given. So stop looking smug.'

'I know,' I said, still smiling.

'Then what are you smiling about?'

'I was trying to imagine what that six-and-a-half-foot hulk and your five-foot-nothing, plump old mother, in her freshly bought knickers, would look like in bed.'

Her face went blank. I thought at first it was anger. And then she giggled. She'd seen it in her mind.

We went back to the kebab place, ordered a fresh lot and ate them this time.

Without the onions.

As it happened we did end up in bed that night. And it was good.

Ten years on, she still lives on the floor above me. 'No favours, please,' she had insisted. 'I'll pay the rent.'

Her kids are in college.

And now and then we still end up in bed, more out of a sense of good manners than anything else. And it's still good.

I'm glad she kept the key.

Harish

When you've played golf every weekend at the Tollygunge Golf Club for twenty-five years, and sometimes mid-week too; and if you've tasted the finest teas your gardens produce week in week out for twenty-five years; and the people you meet at the Tolly or the Saturday Club are the same, day in day out, and the only deviation in your daily routine is the colour of your shirt, it's time to move on.

So one Sunday morning, Harish didn't make it to the Tolly.

After the third telephone call, and this was before seven in the morning, he took his phone off the hook. He rummaged around in his safe, took out all the papers he had, totted up his assets, mostly inherited, partly earned, and discovered he was worth forty-five lakhs. (This was in 1985 when forty-five lakhs meant something).

'Perfect,' he thought. 'Forty-five years old and I'm worth forty-five lakhs.'

An omen.

Seven shirts, seven pants, seven et cetera – of everything he needed fitted neatly into a suitcase he had. He carried it to the door, took one last look at the flat – the cut-glass decanters, the rows of fancy booze bottles, the rosewood furniture, books he'd bought but never read. Things, things and more things he had accumulated over the years. And felt nothing.

Absolutely nothing.

His office watchman in the Timcan's Teas building in Dalhousie Square was surprised to see him on a Sunday evening. Harish gave him an envelope for Mr Prasun Horadia, his boss, and the car keys, picked up his suitcase, walked across to

Chandpal Ghat, took a ferry across the Hooghly to the station and disappeared.

Someone resembling him was seen in the first class compartment of the Bombay Mail via Nagpur. This someone disappeared after Bilaspur junction, and yet no one resembling Harish had got off at Bilaspur.

He was a good-looking bloke. Tall, slim, athletic. He had an aristocratic nose below a pair of bright, intelligent eyes that saw a lot more than they let on. Broad forehead, hair swept back in an outdated Uttam Kumar wave. (We used to tease him about it on the golf course to distract him. 'How long does it take you to get that sweep?' He would smile indulgently at us, and drive the ball three hundred yards along the fairway landing it right where he wanted it to. 'About that long good enough for you?')

I came back and reported to Mr Horadia that I had lost Harish's trail in Bilaspur.

About five years later, I found myself standing on a pavement opposite a modest-looking establishment called '11 to 11' on Wellesley Street. It was about ten forty-five on a Sunday morning. I was on my way home from a round of golf and my car had broken down. I was waiting for the AAEI to come and rescue me. A tall, bald man in a T-shirt was writing the day's menu on a blackboard. A nondescript guy on a cycle drove up.

'Ai Hari! You are needing Rui. Fraysh from my pukur?'

The hand paused over the blackboard, wiped out some words and wrote 'Rui.' He untied the basket from the man's cycle and carried it in to 11 to 11. I saw his reflection in the dark glass window of the restaurant. The softness had disappeared, there was a handlebar moustache and a scar down the right cheek. He was tougher, a bit broader all around, but there was no doubt that it was Harish.

I crossed the road and pushed the door. It was locked.

'Arre Shahib! You cannot read? It opens at eleven,' a voice said behind me.

A couple of people jumped off a tram as it trundled past, and their momentum carried them the four or five steps it took to the entrance where they waited patiently. Their moves seemed practised, as if they had been doing this regularly for some time. I waited with them.

On the dot at eleven, the doors slid open and the five or six patrons hanging around outside walked in. I couldn't. This was not the kind of place I would normally visit. The exterior as I said was modest, nothing to rave about and nothing to complain about either, but the patrons definitely weren't the kind I'd have liked sitting at the next table.

The man from the AAEI arrived in his truck. I crossed the street and handed my keys to him. He popped open the bonnet, and had a look inside. I still had my eyes glued to the entrance of 11 to 11.

'Sorry, sir. Can't fix it here. Have to tow it to the garage,' he said.

'How long will it take?'

'About two to three hours.' He towed the car away.

I hung around on the opposite pavement for half an hour, not sure if I should go in or not. Finally, I crossed the road and walked in.

Clean. But no daylight. It was like stepping into the night. ('At the 11 to 11 it's always night,' I heard later.) There were muted lights. From the outside it looked like it might have six, maybe seven tables. Inside, it was much larger. About twenty tables inside a forty-foot by forty-foot room. The bar, and a damn well-stocked bar at that, completely occupied one wall. Not much conversation was going on. At the first glance, this was a room for serious drinkers. The six or seven people there were immersed in their drinks.

I walked up to the bar, sat on a stool there and looked at Harish. He looked at me. 'What took you so long, Arup?' he asked. 'Not sure you wanted to mix with my clientele? Want a drink? Pink gin? Oh no, of course not. You usually have your first drink on a Sunday at twelve. Still fifteen minutes to go. What dragged *you* away from Tolly this morning?'

This was a different Harish. The one I knew was unfailingly polite and soft-spoken. This one had rejected all the niceties of life. He was blunt to the point of being rude.

'Where the fuck have you been for five years?' I said.

'Right here. And the only rule of this house is that we frown on four-letter words.'

'But ...,' I was getting agitated and he could see that.

He put a pink gin in front of me and in a calm and soothing voice said, 'Here. Break your rule. If you start a few minutes early, the world won't come to an end. Cheers.'

'You chucked it all away for this?'

'Hang around for a couple of hours, and you'll understand why. The phone's in the corner there.'

'Why do I want to know where the phone is?'

'To tell your wife you won't be home for lunch?'

He moved away from me to serve a young man who hadn't taken off his dark glasses and was looking disoriented. He finally took them off, blinked a few times until he got Harish in focus. 'I'll have a beer.'

Harish served him a beer. He took a long swig from his glass, wiped the froth off his mouth and took a photo out of his wallet. He looked at it. And showed it Harish. 'Seen this guy around?'

Harish took a look at the photograph and perhaps he had seen the person, but he returned it with a shake of his head.

'This is my colleague, Ajay. And he's my best friend. Or so I thought. I have to find him or I'll be dead.'

Harish looked across at me. He smiled and raised an eyebrow. 'Was this what you did when you went looking for me?' his expression seemed to say.

'I told him – that bloody Ajay. It wasn't going to work,' the guy with the photograph continued. 'There was absolutely no way he could steal all the secrets from his company and head out to the nearest competitor. He downloaded everything from the main frame. He didn't have to do anything else. It took about four hours. The *entire* exercise took about four hours, that's all.'

The door opened again, letting in a customer and the bright daylight. A stunning lady in her late thirties or early forties walked in. 'I'll have a vodka tonic. Heavy on the ice.'

'Sorry. I can't give you a drink,' replied Harish, going about his business. He didn't even look at the woman.

'I said I'll have a vodka tonic, heavy on the ice. Bring the tonic separately.'

Harish pointed at a sign which said UNESCORTED WOMEN WILL NOT BE SERVED ALCOHOL.

'What do you mean, *no*? Because I'm unescorted? By a man? There isn't a soul here man enough to escort me for crying out loud. Oh dear god in heaven, we in this country still have this colonial hangover of not serving unescorted women! Listen, Hari, the only hangover I want is the one I know I'm going to get after I've had at least six vodka tonics. And for that I'll wait till tomorrow morning. But just now give me a drink.'

Harish refused. She looked around, spotted me and parked herself on the stool next to mine. 'Hi. I'm Shobha. You, dear sir, are now my nominated escort. Can I have that drink now, Hari?'

I was a little perturbed. I'd never been picked up in a bar before. But she obviously knew Harish and was some sort of a regular. Harish brought a drink across for her.

'I'll also have some of that fried pootki maachh instead of these boring peanuts,' she said, pushing back the bowl he'd brought with him. She emptied her glass in one gulp, chased it down with a tonic and before she'd put the tonic down, her fresh vodka had arrived with a plate full of small fish, about an inch and a half long, fried golden. It was obviously a ritual both Shobha and Harish were familiar with.

Harish went back to the man with the photograph, who was saying, 'It took the office about an hour to find him out, and bang, he ends up with a prosecution case that is going to take years and years to come to court. And, in the meantime, he's somewhere here spending all the money that the competitors paid him. He's just dropped off the face of the earth.' He leaned across to Shobha and showed her the photograph. 'Say madam, have you seen him? This is what he looks like. No? Well, this is what he looked like. Maybe he's grown a beard. Maybe he's changed colour. Who the fuck knows?'

'Sir,' Harish said, 'I'll forgive you this transgression, but I frown upon the eff word being used in this establishment.'

'But you know what, I'm his boss – so I have to take the rap. *Bring him back*, they said, *or don't come back*. Hey I'm a desk jockey. You tell me to find out anything in the ether, it will take me next to no time. But Jesus! Actually, physically looking for something in the world, with all its people and its muck and dirt and traffic … who wants to know … I don't care about what happens outside my four walls – walls I haven't seen in the last few weeks. God, I miss the clean white walls of my office. You know, the only coloured thing in my room is my monitor. Everything else is pristine white. Oh yes, there is a sign on my wall. It says, in black on white, just a single word. THIMK! Good, isn't it? THIMK! Did you get it? Tee-aitch-eye-em-kay. The em instead of the en makes you think. Doesn't it?'

Shobha looked at him as if he was something that had crawled out of the woodwork.

'You're still using that old IBM poster in your office? Passé baby, passé!'

'Anyway, you know what they said to me last week? They said if I didn't find him within this week, they were going to cut my daily allowance. If I didn't find him within the week after, they'd cancel my return fare. If I didn't find him by the week after, I'd be fired. Time's running out for me. Give me another drink. If only I could find him. I want my life back.'

Harish put another bottle of beer in front of him.

'Last month I was a happy man. Dedicated to everything I did. To my parents, to my company, to my fiancée. What have I got now? Sweet fucking nothing.'

Harish looked at him disapprovingly, but decided to let it pass. The man was obviously disturbed about something.

'I've got a company breathing down my neck, parents who are worried sick and a fiancée who, if I don't get back to her immediately, will dump me before you can say surf the Net. Give me a drink I said. Oh, you did. Well, give me another. Yeah yeah yeah. I'll pay. Jesus, you're worse than the computer games I design. Pay and play. Pay and play. Every game has a built-in program saying pay and play. Just like you. Who the fuck wrote your software, pal?'

Harish leaned below the counter, took out a 7 iron golf club, returned the man's money, poured the man's drink into the sink and asked him to leave. Very politely. The man was about to get belligerent and was readying himself for battle. But he focussed on Harish and gave up. It was a no contest. He left.

'Still pretty good with the 7 iron I see,' I said. He smiled. And his smile grew wider as a shaft of daylight let in an elderly gentleman in his early seventies or thereabouts, dressed in a white dhoti-panjabi.

'The usual, my good man. Soda and bitters and easy on the ice.'

'Arre Biren Babu. Aapni? You don't usually grace us with your presence on Sundays. Welcome.'

He walked up to me, looked at me through his thick lenses and, with a benign expression, said, 'You, young man, are obviously a fresher.'

'Er ... yes, sir. Fresher?'

'Your clothes, sir, are a giveaway, and only a fresher would have the temerity to occupy a place that has been held in reserve for me for the last four years.'

Harish was ready with his drink.

'Arup, this is Biren Babu. You're going to have to move. Biren Babu, this is Arup, a ghost from my past.'

'Ah! That explains the clothes,' said Biren Babu. 'Straight from Tolly, perhaps?'

Harish stifled his laughter as he moved away. A waitress entered from the kitchen with a tray full of small cashew nut servings and placed them in front of everybody. She was very gentle with some old customers. Others, who tried to pinch her bottom, were put in their place.

One customer got up and walked up to a jukebox. God, I hadn't seen one in years! Trust Harish to find one. The customer chose John Coltrane's *Lush Life*. It's a sad piece of music and the surrounding restaurant sounds turned quiet for the duration.

The hours passed. A whole lot of people came, had their drinks and food, but very few left without sharing some confidence or the other with Harish. He listened to them patiently and never offered a word of advice or encouragement. He just listened.

That afternoon Harish was as much of a stranger to me as were all his customers. He'd often catch me looking at him with a puzzled expression and would shrug or smile. I was by now into my nth pink gin and was beginning to feel them a bit. From the kitchen a plateful of freshly fried rui maachh arrived with a bowl full of kashundi on the side, some sliced onions and lemons and a plateful of fried green chillies.

Biren Babu, Shobha and I dug into them with gusto.

'Arup? Did Hari call you Arup?' Shobha asked, wiping a bit of kashundi off her upper lip with her tongue. 'Well, since you're my escort you might as well listen to me. I feel like a man in a wheelchair. I am a woman, all my faculties intact, with more brains in my little finger than most men in their skulls I know. But … I am a woman. So everyone around treats me like a handicapped person. Every time a woman tries to stand on her own two feet, there are millions who bring her crashing down. What a life!'

Hari put another drink down in front of her. She reached out for her bag. He stopped her.

'This one's on me,' he said.

'Are you going to sit here all morning? Sipping a soda and bitters? How utterly depressing!' Shobha told Biren Babu.

'And all afternoon and all evening,' he replied cheerfully. 'Occasionally, I reward myself with some snacks, such as this and continue with this one glass of soda and bitters until this fine inn keeper downs the shutters or throws me out.'

Biren Babu turned away from Shobha and looked longingly at all the bottles behind the bar. He licked his lips and his hand quivered slightly as he sipped the bitters and soda.

'Madam, if you have any objections to what I consume, I

would request you to kindly find another place to sit. But you must take the trouble to understand that the reason I sit here is that I get what photographers call a wide angle view of the contents of the bar. When I say bar, I mean a bar … where every nectar-like drink is available. Not just nectar but nectar for the gods. I should know because what's there in that array of bottles behind Harish, has at some time or the other in my life, passed through my lips. Not just those but drinks you haven't even heard of. I can taste some of them, you know, even now – especially when I'm asleep.'

He helped himself to another piece of fish, ignored the kashundi, placed a slice of onion on the fish, squeezed a drop of lemon on it and popped it into his mouth, dipped a fried green chilli into a small bowl of salt and bit into it. Sheer bliss spread across his face.

'Yes, this is a serious bar,' he continued after he had swallowed the food. 'And I like it even though the doctors, those ignorant quacks, said I couldn't drink any more. "One more and we are not responsible for what happens", they said pompously. This was just after they'd injected me with something or the other. The doctors think they are gods. My friend who was in the hospital had a bottle of the finest whisky with him. I ignored the doctor and I took a sip. And I gagged. The first meal I'd ever had, anno prashoner bhaat, came up. Believe me. The first solid meal I must have had when I was what, about two months old? I could taste it. And the doctor stood there, another syringe in his hand, and waited for the heaving to get worse. He jammed the needle in me until the shuddering of my body stopped.

'You knew this would happen,' I accused him. 'Why did you let me drink?'

'Would you have obeyed me?' he said in his superior educated fashion and left the hospital room.

'I guess not. But since then all I ever have is bitters and soda. Just one that keeps me going.'

Harish looked at him indulgently.

Biren Babu had a knife and a lemon in front of him. He cut a thin slice of lemon and put it in his glass. The few remaining bubbles of soda wrapped themselves around the lemon. He looked at the knife longingly.

Harish came up to him and took the knife from his hands very gently.

'See, Madam? How well Harish understands me. No sharp instruments are kept within my limited reach for more than a few seconds.'

'You know, Arup sir and Miss Shobha, you know what they say? They say the worst thing that can befall a man is to be there at the cremation of his son.'

He bit into a chilli. I noticed his eyes were watering. Was it the chilli or were they watering before?

'Damn strong chilli,' he said. 'Oh sorry, Miss Shobha, please excuse my language.' He took a sip of water and started singing softly in Bengali.

Not very loudly. More to himself than to us.

He came in one evening
He came in with the tide.

He told me 'bout his daughter
And his son who had died.

Their mother is heartbroken
And she just wants to die.
'Cause there's no one there to listen
To her night-time lullabies.

'You know something, Arup Moshai ... after performing the last rites of one's grandchildren, cremating one's son is not too difficult a task. It is child's play,' he said in a matter-of-fact way.

Both Shobha and I looked shocked. He wondered at the expression on our faces and thought about what he had just said.

'Perhaps my selection of words was unfortunate. Ai je Harish! I don't suppose you'd give me a glass of dry white wine, would you?'

'That will be thirty for the soda and bitters and forty-six rupees for the wine,' Harish said.

'Forty-six rupees? You mean to say if I had forty-six rupees you would actually serve me a glass of wine? Knowing that it would probably kill me? God, you are a cold-hearted bastard, Harish. Again, Miss Shobha, my apologies. What is happening to me? My tongue seems to be remembering words I thought it had long stopped using. Harish? Have you, by chance, been mixing whisky in my bitters and soda?'

Lunch had come and gone. At tea-time instead of tea, we had some vodka on ice with lots of prawns.

The door opened, letting in some noise from the traffic. I noticed it was getting dark outside. A group of noisy youngsters entered, demanded a place, were told all the tables were reserved and were escorted out by Harish and his 7 iron.

Harish went off to welcome someone else who'd occupied a table near the juke box. He came back, poured a soda for himself and a single malt for the customer, and went to sit with him. I watched them for a little while. The man was animatedly telling Harish something that had Harish in splits of laughter. I wished I could be a straw in the straw holder, listening to what the man was saying. I'd never seen Harish in all the years we'd worked together laugh so unabashedly at anything. He got up and came back to the bar.

'The biggest culprit, of course, is my husband,' Shobha said. 'Have you met him? How could you have? But let me tell you, you've met hundreds like him. You might even be like him yourself. All understanding, all liberal, supporting women's causes at the drop of a panty. But when it comes to a wife? Ha!' She knocked back the dregs in her glass, swirled the ice around looking at it morosely. She was angry. 'All the bleeding-heart liberalism goes right out of the window. Here I am – an MBA from one of the biggest management colleges in the world, reduced to being a wife – and a mother to his children. Hey, I've got nothing against my children. They are the cutest kids I've ever come across, if I say so myself. But surely there is more to life than breeding and being a milch cow? Thank god they've grown up and are in university now. Otherwise I'd be going round the bend on a one-way street to hell. Sorry, I mix my metaphors when I'm into my ... what is this, my seventh vodka?'

'Eighth, actually, but who's counting?' Harish said, smiling.

'What are you smiling about?' Biren Babu who had tuned out during Shobha's lament, asked. 'That's not a happy-to-see-the-back-of-me smile. That's a knowing, cunning smile. Ah, I see now. You were trying the reverse psychology bit on me, were you? You knew if you'd refused me a libation I would have demanded my rights and fought for it. Or left in a huff. This way you keep me here, and every day I come and spend my thirty-six rupees on bitters and soda. Smart thinking, smart thinking. Either way I don't get a drink. You know? A drink drink.'

'Eighth, you said?' Shobha asked Harish. He nodded.

'I'd better get the hell out of here,' she slurred as she got off the stool. 'How much do I owe you?'

'I'll put it on your tab. Is your driver with you?' Harish asked, concerned.

'Always dear Harish, always, when I visit the 11 to 11. See you next Sunday.'

She turned at the doorway and looked at us. 'Biren Babu, will you be here next Sunday?'

'If I'm not here in person, Harish has promised to keep my ashes in an urn on top of the refrigerator.'

She walked out of there, ramrod straight. If I hadn't seen her down eight drinks, I never would have believed that she was plastered.

It was a quarter to eleven at night. The day had gone by really fast. Dozens of people had walked into the 11 to 11 and walked out happier – not just with the drinks, but they had been made to feel important enough to be heard. Harish who used to be a loner when we worked together had become good at that.

But perhaps he always had been and we just hadn't noticed it, so wrapped up we were in our careers, our ambitions and the games we played.

I had met all sorts of men and women, different kinds of people in the last twelve hours than I had in the last dozen years. Some came, downed a couple or two, had a quick word and went out in a better frame of mind. Others like Shobha, Biren Babu and me stayed as long as we could.

It was just Harish, Biren Babu and I now.

'You know, when I started frequenting this fine establishment, all my friends laughed at me,' Biren Babu said. 'The doctors were appalled at the fact that I was going to fight my alcoholism by coming here every evening. You must have guessed by now, Arup Moshai, that I am an alcoholic. But I figure I haven't been doing too badly. How long has it been since I've been coming here? I'll tell you. Four years and twenty-two days. They said if I came here I'd die within the week. But here I am. Still going strong. On my soda and bitters. Most times one an evening is quite satisfactory. And if I'm feeling really reckless, two, but always only soda and bitters.'

The door opened. I ignored the late entry. I was watching Biren Babu closely, hanging on to every word he said.

'Remember that movie? In which this man has forty spears sticking out of him and his friend asks him if it hurts? And he replies only when I laugh. No, no. Was it a movie or did I read it in a book?' Biren Babu looked confused. He was beginning to look tired. He had been there right from the beginning of the day and must have been exhausted.

I felt an arm around my shoulders. Surprised, I turned around. It was my wife.

'How did you get here?' I whispered.

'Harish phoned me hours ago,' she said smiling. 'He said about now would be a good time to collect you.'

'Thanks Harish,' I said. 'Biren Babu, this is my wife. She has come to take me home.'

He got off his stool and shook my wife's hand. 'I had a family once,' he said. 'I had a home and a job and a life. All of it went down the bottle. But that's another story. There was so much happiness and so much grief. I hope my wife is happy wherever she is, my son wherever he is and my grandchildren.'

He looked at the last few drops of his soda and bitters. 'You know, Arup Moshai, drowning in the ocean is easy, but it is impossible to drown one's memories in a soda and bitters.'

He bowed to us and made for the exit, stopped at the door, opened it and turned. There was nothing dramatic in the way he spoke. He was just reporting a fact. 'I can't watch sunsets any more. It's much easier for me sitting here surrounded by darkness than it is watching a sunset. A red sun descending into the water shimmering. It's amazing, the contrast. Of colours, of speed. It takes hours for the sun to move across the sky. And then it comes near the ocean and plunges in at such speed! As if it wants to drown. In a hurry. Painlessly. Often I'd stick my nose into a glass while the sun was hovering over the horizon. I'd look up and it was gone. One of these days, I guess, when I can't hold on any longer, I'll go to Goa, walk across to the beach at sunset, and take one last look at the sun. I'll put my nose into a glass of single malt while the sun shimmers over the ocean. Take a long sip. And I'll look up. And the sun will be gone. And so will I.'

He slipped out of the door.

'A dry martini for your wife, one final single malt for you and my first and last cognac for the day,' Harish said turning to my wife.

'You remembered what I used to drink?' my wife looked surprised.

'Many years ago, you taught me how to make the best one.'

We raised our glasses in a silent toast.

'See you next Sunday, Harish,' I said as my wife and I got ready to leave.

'Golf?' my wife asked.

It was the first time in years I hadn't *thought* of golf.

Zack's

The doorbell rang. I opened it and there, dressed in flamingo pink and diamonds to match, stood a tall, slightly androgynous creature. Her pallu had slipped onto her arm. She was taller than me by about six inches and while my eyes were fixed on her remarkable cleavage, my jaw was scraping the floor.

'Close your mouth young man, and do not covet that which you cannot haveth. It says so in the Bible. Besides you're too young. Tell your holy mother Sati G is here.' She sailed past me, the Battleship Potem-pink.

This was in 1971. East Pakistan had voted to become Bangladesh, Pakistan had declared war, and the Sindhi Ladies Association of Calcutta had decided to do its bit. Every time there was a flood, famine, riot, war or any calamity, the SLA would swing into action. And since we had a rather large house, the meetings would take place there. Sindhi women of every hue and precious gem would walk in to attend these meetings.

Namoo Aunty with her bulbous green eyes and emeralds to match would be the first to arrive, ostensibly to help my mother organize the action – but actually to take over it completely. Chitra Aunty, in a simple white sari with costume jewellery, would be next. Mrs Lalchand, the jeweller's wife, came dressed in a georgette sari and no jewels. 'Ask the papadwali if she eats papad,' she said. 'She doesn't. So I don't wear jewellery.' Mohini's favourites were sapphires. And so on.

All the usual suspects were there that day, and planning began in full swing and loudly. I had been commanded by my mother to make sure there was a steady supply of water, tea and samosas throughout the morning, and to answer the doorbell.

Sati G was 'persona non G' in my mother's circle of friends and when people spoke of her, they spoke in hushed tones. The reason? She was ... well, 'dishonourable' would be the closest translation of the word in Sindhi. In Sindhi it had much stronger connotations.

The meeting came to a sudden halt. I think even the birds stopped chattering outside in the garden. Sati G wasn't invited anywhere, but she knew she would always be welcome at my mother's, a firm believer in 'atithi devo bhava' and completely non-judgmental about people. She said hello to everybody in the room.

No one replied, except my mother – who greeted her warmly and offered her a chair.

'No Dadi (everyone called my mother that), I've just come to donate this bangle to the war effort. The courts have blocked all my accounts.'

Collective gasp in room.

At the diamonds on the bangle or her blocked accounts, I never found out.

'Stay,' said my mother. 'Have a cup of tea.'

'No Dadi,' she said, looking around the room. 'I have enough cats of my own to deal with.'

I fell in love with her right there, at that moment. I would've liked to describe what happened in the room after she left, but it would suffice to say there was pandemonium.

I was sixteen. And she became an obsession. I had to find out everything I could about her. My parents were reticent about her. My sisters and brother couldn't be bothered. Who do I ask?

I lurked outside her nightclub, Zack's, for many evenings, waiting to catch a glimpse of her. Of course, no one had told me there was a back door to the place and she used that door only. Not even the police knew about it.

Saturday was 'Sailors' Night' and inevitably ended in a brawl with knives being flashed around. The police used to park themselves just outside, waiting for the first sign of trouble which was, more often than not, a bloodied man hurtling out of the bar. And the raid would follow. It usually ended in about fifteen minutes. Zack's was declared closed for the night, and the police would drive away with a Black Maria police van full of drunken sailors. Half an hour later the place would open again.

Was Zack's reputation, and the fact that she owned it, the reason for the cats' dislike of her? There was no way I was going to get in to Zack's on my own to find out.

Raju was our cricket captain. And if he was to be believed, he'd seen and done it all. Monday morning I dropped into his shop and asked him to step outside, pretending I wanted to discuss some cricket strategy. His father looked at me disapprovingly. We settled down at a tea stall, and I laid my cards on the table. 'I have to meet Sati G. Help!'

'Bhenchod, you mad or what!'

'Yaar, there is no one else I know who can get me into her Zack's. You've been there. Come on.'

'Go to hell! You're underage.'

'Come on, Raju! Okay, just tell me where she lives. I'll go to her on my own. You don't have to come.'

'No one knows where she lives.'

'Then get me into Zack's.'

'Fuck off. With your luck, your dad will find out. He'll tell my dad. And then I'll be dead.'

After much cajoling (Raju, I have no one else in the world), threatening (I'll walk out of the team if you don't), bribery and corruption (I'll give you eight hours a week extra at the nets), he agreed.

'Okay, bugger, but please – huh – wear long pants and not shorts.'

I never did make it into Zack's.

There we were on Wednesday evening. I was dressed in my brother's clothes, without his knowledge, choking on a cigarette (a useful prop if you want to look older, but not if you're choking), trying to look as if I belonged.

And that was the one day Sati G decided to drive up through the front gate at Zack's, spotted Raju and me waiting to get in, got a couple of bouncers to bundle us into her car, dropped Raju home, and glowered at me all the way to my place.

We stopped outside my door.

'If you walk past Zack's, make sure you do it on the other pavement. Anywhere near, and I take you straight to your holy mother. Is that understood?'

'Aunty, why don't you come in now and tell her?'

If looks could kill.

'Aunty, Zack's doesn't interest me, you do. I wanted to meet you. But no one would tell me where you lived. My "holy mother" would understand. I think. I hope.'

'Beta, you're much too young for me, and I have too much respect for your mother. Anyway, you've met me. Now go.'

'No.'

'Arre! Get out before my driver throws you out.'

'Do it. Throw me out.'

By now, surprised at the occupants still sitting inside, after so much time, a curious crowd had gathered around the car.

'Driver,' she gave me a long, hard look. 'Gari chalao.'

And we left the scene.

'Where to, memsaab?'

'Hastings. Nadi ke kinare.'

We drove along for a while in silence.

'What do you want from me?' she asked.

'I want to know why my mother's "cats" don't like you.'

Her lips cracked into a smile – the first one that evening. We reached the river. She sent the driver away for a stroll. And then, a couple of hours later, around midnight, she dropped me home.

'You are never to meet me again. Not a word about this to anyone until I'm dead. You've promised.'

I got out of the car and shook her hand. The car drove away. I never saw her again.

But at that moment there was hell waiting at home. This was a time before cell phones so there was no way I could have informed them that I was going to be late or where I was. All they had heard from the sniggering, nosy neighbours was that I had been driven away in a car by Sati G. 'Oooh! Your son went out with Sati G!'

It was pleasant to know that my parents had been worried more about my sudden, long absence from home, than the fact that I had been out with Sati G. They never asked me what had happened. I never told them. However, I was grounded for the rest of the month, dying to tell a story I had promised never to tell.

'I don't have much time,' Sati G said, as we drove off towards the riverside. 'I have to be back at Zack's by midnight. If I'm not there, there will be chaos. If they know I'm not present, even the customers don't behave themselves.' She paused, suddenly snapping out of her thoughts, and turned to look at me. 'So what do you want to know about me?'

I wondered where I should begin. What did I want to know? 'My mother mentioned in passing, that you made quite a dramatic exit from Karachi …'

Karachi. That's when she sighed, adjusted her hair with her fingers and, staring at the water, began her story.

On Boxing Day, every year, Vishnu Gulabrai started planning the next Christmas bash. Every successive party always outdid the previous one. Vishnu Gulabrai was larger than life. He had more than doubled his fortune supplying uniforms to the British Army in World War II. His trading empire stretched from his home base in Karachi to every corner of the country and to most corners of the British Empire. The Brits loved him but they also laughed at him, at his attempts to be more Brit than the Brits. 'They paid me thirty per cent more than the market rate for the uniforms so they can laugh all they want,' he said. He was feared and revered as a boss, and loved and envied as a host. And Boxing Day 1946 was going to be his last party in undivided India.

Sati, his daughter, sat in front of her dressing table, applying the finishing touches to her make-up, not that she needed any. She stood up and twirled in front of the full-length mirror. She liked what she saw – a beautiful young girl in a dark silk sarong skirt and a midriff top, linked together by a metal ring, with just a hint of the midriff showing. She was wearing a dress she'd seen Lauren Bacall wearing in *To Have and Have Not*. She'd drawn the design from memory and had her durzee create a near-perfect replica. This was a style that would become a fashion statement about thirty years later. But that day in 1946, in all of Karachi, it was one of a kind.

She knew that when she paused at the top of the grand staircase, before descending to the ballroom, for a few seconds all eyes would be riveted on her. Just to revel in those few seconds of complete adoration would make the whole effort that had gone into creating this look, worth it.

No. One. Noticed. Her.

She stood there for a full half-minute, looking down at a sea of troubled heads, all deeply immersed in conversation. Stray words floated up to her. 'Partition ... riots ... Calcutta ... schism ... blood demands blood ... Delhi ... chop them up into pieces ...'

Her father, with his mop of white hair, was moving from group to group, seemed more worried than the rest.

She stood at the top of the stairs and shivered. One person detached himself from the crowd and came rushing up the stairs, panting slightly from the climb, looked admiringly at her. 'How on earth did you manage to get your hands on a Milo Anderson original?' he gasped.

'What?' she said, flustered.

'This dress. It's one of a kind, made especially for …'

'Lauren Bacall, I know. I copied it and had it stitched by the neighbourhood durzee. Who are you?' she asked, amused that a total stranger, a man, should be so interested in her dress, and so knowledgeable about its antecedents.

'Allow me to introduce myself,' he said. 'I am Benjamin Zachariah, a friend of your father's. Visiting from Bombay. Will you do me the honour of letting me be your escort for the evening?'

She looked at him quizzically. He looked much too young to be her father's friend, and a little too old to be her escort. She was a bit annoyed, but he was the only one who had noticed her, and he did seem to be informed on today's fashions. She put her hand on his arm, nodded, and together they made their way down the grand staircase.

She was completely ignorant of the fact that there were changes taking place all over the country. Gandhi was fasting his way to freedom, Jinnah was malignant (quite literally, as we would learn later) about Pakistan, the whole sub-continent was planning a splendid send-off for the British, and like all the guests there she too was completely unaware of what was soon to follow. She was in good company.

Benjamin took charge of her that evening. He never left her side. Anyone watching them would think he was the host and she the guest. The ease with which he included her in all the conversations, his effortless repartee, the attention he paid her, all contributed to a level of enjoyment she'd never had at any of her father's parties. From being the 'pretty little daughter' she had graduated to an acceptable adult. And, for the first time in her life, people listened to what she had to say, instead of just admiring her ensemble. She loved every moment of it.

Except the moments when Partition was discussed. And there were many such. Half the people at the party were planning to decamp from Karachi, and the other half were dying to buy them out. Sati had never encountered such conversations before. They had an unpleasant edge to them. Even though was she enjoying herself, at moments like these, she felt distinctly uncomfortable. At her father's party? It surprised her, this was a first.

She was bewildered when Sayyed Uncle asked 'Sati beti, where do you plan to stay after Partition? This side or that side?'

'This side or that side of what?' she replied. 'My grandmother used to say she was born in Clifton and she would die here. I intend on following in her footsteps.'

'You just might,' one of the guests, Abida Begum, said. 'Sooner than you think.'

Benjamin could feel her tremble. Was it anger? Or worry? He didn't wait to find out as he whisked her away from there. 'Let's go out to the garden for a bit of fresh air.'

Sati followed. On the way they bumped into Sati's father.

'Ah, you found each other. Good. After the party, I want to talk to both of you. See you in the library.' He rushed away to take care of newly-arrived guests.

They sat in the small 'orchard', overlooking the sea. She was disturbed. He was solicitous.

'What happened in there just now?' she asked. 'Why was Abida, who is normally the gentlest person I know, suddenly so vicious?'

'It's in the air, Sati,' Benjamin said quietly. 'There is a vast churning going on, a great samudra manthan. Your friends? Your foes? Which is which? Soon no one will be able to tell.'

'And you my new-found friend, will you also turn out to be a foe?' she enquired, looking like a vulnerable child.

'I shall protect you with my life,' he answered, half in jest with a courtly bow straight out of a period Hollywood film.

She smiled – reassured by his humour and grace.

'If you're a friend of Baba's, how is it that we've never met before?'

'I saw you last when you were four, I think. I haven't been to Karachi in years, but Vishnu and I have been in touch. We write long letters to each other about life and business. Business mostly. He asked me to be here today, saying he had something to discuss in person, so I set sail from Bombay in a friend's yacht about a week ago. And here I am.'

'You know, I've never been on a yacht.'

'That wrong can be righted soon,' he said.

'How did you know so much about my dress?'

'The designer, Milo, wrote to me and asked if I knew of a

fabric that would fall correctly. I sent him a sample from one of my suppliers. It worked.'

She smiled. A light sea breeze carried the scent of limes and mandarin oranges. For an hour or so they sat there and talked about everything from fabrics to society. Well, he talked. She listened. And she learnt a lot more in that hour about Karachi, India and the post-war world.

'Shall we go in?' he suggested. 'The guests should be ready to leave by now. Time to say your goodbyes.'

'I don't feel like it. I'd much rather sit here and listen to you.'

He didn't insist and they watched the guests leave one by one. With the last one gone, they made their way back slowly, reluctantly to the house and the meeting with her father in the library.

It was a man's room. No frills. Books lined all the walls, from the floor up to the ceiling. A corner of the room was lit by a lamp. On a trolley under the lamp, there was an array of cut-glass decanters. And trying to pour himself a drink from one of them stood Sati's father. His hands shook. The drink spilt all over the place. Benjamin rushed up to him and took the decanter gently from his hands.

'Here, let me do that, Mr Gulabrai.'

'Thank you, Benjamin, thank you. Ah, Sati! There you are. No, no. Let it be,' he said, as she picked up his discarded dinner jacket off the floor. 'I'll have little use for that in the future.'

He took a long sip from his glass, settled down on his chair and looked vacantly into the distance. His hands had stopped shaking, but he still wasn't in control. Sati had seen him like this only once before – when her mother had died suddenly and rather senselessly, infected by a paper cut.

This was not nervousness or fear that she was looking at. This was a quiet rage. He emptied the contents of his glass, and held it out to Benjamin who refilled it.

'Baba, are you sure you've had enough?' she asked sarcastically.

'Beta, now there's a line I've been waiting to hear all my life. I have absolutely no intentions of leaving this fine whisky behind for some unpadh philistine who won't appreciate it.'

'Where are you going?'

'Oh Sati, Sati, my innocent little Sati, what are we going to do with you?' he said looking very depressed and concerned.

Benjamin and Sati exchanged looks. Both of them were worried. She had never seen her father maudlin. Drunk? Yes. Sardonic? Always. Maudlin? Never.

'You know,' he said after taking another sip, 'my Muslim friends can't wait to get their hands on my land and my home; my Hindu friends can't wait for me to fall flat on my face; and my English Christian friends resent me for throwing a better Christmas party than they ever can. And these are my friends. I wonder what my enemies think.' He had that familiar sardonic look in his eye that Sati recognized. 'People of all religions dislike me. Does that mean I'm secular?'

He was slowly regaining control over himself. Though much relieved, Sati was still a bit worried about him. All was not right with the world yet.

'And you, my Jewish friend. What about you?'

'I'm afraid it will take Moses' staff, the one he parted the Red

Sea with, to pry me away from you. Just don't throw a Hanukkah party, nu!' Benjamin replied with an exaggerated shrug.

'We had a quiet laugh,' Sati G reminisced. 'Benjamin was good at that. I miss him so. You know, once he helped me set up here, after the initial years of struggle, he went to Israel to look for his roots.' She looked out of the car window at a steamboat chugging down the river. 'I wish he would return. I need a laugh or two.'

'We need to get out of here. We need a plan. And no one in Karachi must get even a whiff of it,' said her father, looking gravely at the two faces in front of him. He was not joking.

Sati was perturbed. She couldn't imagine life anywhere except in Karachi. 'Baba, you want us to leave Clifton? I'm not going to do that. This is home. How can we …? Surely, no one will harm us?'

'Didn't you hear what was going on at the party? You know what Ghulam Ahmed told me? He said, as much as he loved our family, there was little he would be able to do for us. For generations our families have been friends and partners. But once that line is drawn, in the eyes of everybody, we will be just another Hindu family. I'm willing to wager everything I have that conversations like that one are taking place every day in Bombay, Calcutta, Delhi, Agra.'

Sati was amazed. And unconvinced. 'We can't leave everything and just … go.'

'We have to. We don't have a choice. But we are not going to leave anything behind. That's why I invited Benjamin, my old young friend, to help.'

'Benjamin? You are a part of this?' she asked.

Benjamin nodded.

Vishnu walked up to a safe in the wall and brought out a sheaf of paper. 'These are details of my businesses around the country and in some parts of the world. Europe has been a disaster over the last few years because of the war, but the rest is pretty solid. Benjamin, along with his partners, has managed my businesses overseas from Aden. He has been a valued partner and friend. Over the next three months I want to convert all this into cash. It will be a strenuous task but with Benjamin and his companies helping, not an impossible one. There is a major snag though.'

'One!' Sati exclaimed. 'I see the road ahead littered with snags.'

'Secrecy. No one in Karachi must know what is happening.'

Benjamin looked worried. 'That's going to be tough.'

'I discovered this evening that many of my powerful friends aren't friends at all. If they get a whiff of what we are planning, they'll come down on us like a pack of hyenas ripping out bits and pieces of my businesses for themselves.'

He paced about the room. Now that he was planning something, now that he had someone to share his exit ideas with, he was the Vishnu of old that Benjamin knew, the enthusiastic father that Sati knew.

'There is only one way we are going to keep their noses out of my business. We have to create a believable diversion that will keep their minds and noses occupied.'

'And what will that be?' she said. 'Any ideas?'

'Yes, just one. While Benjamin and I work behind the scenes, you and he will be working right in full view of all of Karachi.'

'Doing what, exactly?'

Vishnu looked out of the window at nothing in particular – trying to work out, perhaps, the best way he could tell her what she was supposed to do. Benjamin got up and picked up a book from a shelf. He turned the pages without actually reading anything.

'Sati beti,' Vishnu said, as he put his arm around her and led her to the window. 'If we don't do this, we stand to lose everything, perhaps even our lives. What I have construed from the things I've heard tonight, well … once the Partition occurs, our lives won't be worth a khota rupaiya.'

Very gently, he told her what he wanted from her and Benjamin.

She froze, shrugged his arms off her shoulders and looked pensive. She stared out of the window at the moon, and then looked down at the orchard where she and Benjamin had sat earlier in the evening. Benjamin was caring, protective and quite a raconteur. She wasn't too sure she would be able to get through it, but she was sure it wouldn't be boring.

It was insane. No one was going to fall for it. Or were they? Benjamin and she were going to act out a kind of Baron Munchausen fantasy that even the Baron himself would find hard to believe.

'If we all play our parts with complete conviction, I promise you, dear daughter of mine, we will get away from this unscathed.'

She walked up to Benjamin and looked him straight in the eye.

'Benjamin? Are you okay with this?'

'If it must be done, it must be done.'

Sati and Benjamin partied across the city, arm in arm. There wasn't a soiree they did not attend. Karachi was amazed at the whirlwind romance happening in front of their eyes, not to mention aghast.

'How could an older Jewish man dare to woo the young daughter of one of Karachi's leading citizens?'

'Shameless hussy.'

'He's old enough to be her father.'

'Did you see that ring? Wonder what she did to get it.'

'Look at those diamond cuff links. He must have done something really special.'

'He's bought her a car. '

'Shameless hussy.'

'Oooh! They were holding hands in public!'

'Did you see the lipstick marks on him?'

'If they're like this out in the open, I wonder what's happening in private.'

'Shameless hussy.'

Sayyed Uncle, one of their closest family friends, was the first to drop them. Word had spread about his displeasure with the couple and the family. And, when they went to his haveli to a dinner to which they had been invited, they were denied entry by an apologetic gatekeeper. He said the party had been cancelled. The fact that there were about forty cars in the driveway was a big embarrassment for this old-school khidmatgar. But they left, uncomplaining.

Notandas, a prominent trader in Karachi, spoke to Mr Gulabrai and told him neither he nor his daughter was welcome in his shop. 'No shame is coming to you? Letting a daughter of our revered Sindhi community dance around Karachi with a yehudi? You are cutting our noses!'

'What am I to do?' Mr Gulabrai asked. 'You are a senior member of the Sindhi community. She is my only child. I cannot say no to her. Perhaps you can give me some advice?' he said, and rushed away without waiting for an answer. He wasn't seen for some time after that.

Karachi was a cosmopolitan city, a bustling metropolis with a real khichdi of communities living side by side with of course the British, all equally proud that they were its citizens. Karachi was the cultural capital of the Raj in India with values and traditions much respected by all of them. Often it was described as Europe of the East.

Benjamin and Sati went their merry way, scandalizing communities across the board. Nothing was sacrosanct. In a matter of weeks, there wasn't a community or tradition that wasn't in some way, upset by Sati and Benjamin. Things were simmering, almost brought to their boiling point. Polite society in Karachi was about to declare war on the two. 'The minute Vishnu Gulabrai comes back from his tours, we'll send him an ultimatum. Tell them to behave or they'll be ostracized.'

Mr Gulabrai had been busy travelling the length and breadth of the country, visiting all his outlets, meeting his business contacts, spreading confidence in the future wherever he went, playing an elaborate game of chess with himself. One wrong move and he'd checkmate himself.

When he did come back to Karachi, he stayed out of sight, closeted with Benjamin, pouring over numbers, dispatching messengers to places far and wide, using the yacht's radio service instead of the government postal or telegraph services to do his business.

Once everything was in place as he had planned, three months after Christmas, Karachi high society, ready to take stern action against Sati and Benjamin, was in for the surprise of its life.

They had barely finished their morning cups of tea. Kids were being readied for school, teeth were still being brushed. As they opened their morning papers, out popped a gilt-edged invitation, perhaps the first incident of a newspaper delivering more than the news. It was a wedding invitation, engraved with the name of the recipient on the envelope.

It was a credit to Mr Gulabrai's organizing capabilities that the right invitations reached the right people. There were no mix-ups. Sati and Benjamin were to be 'joined in holy matrimony on 15 March 1947.'

Outrage made way for delight. All of Karachi loved a party. A wedding was even better. A wedding that joined the scandalous couple was the best. It solved a lot of problems. Now they wouldn't have to take any action against the two. The earlier bitchy remarks made way for charitable ones.

'A spring-weds-summer marriage! So romantic.'

'They could have been a bit more discreet.'

'But they do make a handsome couple.'

Of course Abida Begum made sure that she made her

remark within Sati's earshot, 'She must be pregnant. Why else the hurry, no?'

By and large, all ill-will and prejudices forgotten, they came in droves, blessed Sati and Benjamin, and had a splendid time.

'Mr Gulabrai,' one of Vishnu's guests said solicitously, 'you don't look too well.'

'It's nothing,' Vishnu replied hastily, brushing him away. 'Just planning Sati's wedding. Exhausting business. You know how it is …'

The guests partied late into the night. Except for Ghulam Ahmed Ubaidullah and family that had come all the way from Larkana, and were staying the night, all went away satisfied that society as they knew it had survived.

It was a tradition in Karachi that on the morning after the wedding, breakfast was an open house affair. Everybody was welcome. The first few guests that arrived late the next morning were welcomed by the Ubaidullahs. Vishnu, Sati and Benjamin were nowhere to be seen.

'You won't be seeing them,' said Mr Ubaidullah. 'They left this place last night after the ceremonies.'

'Where have they gone?'

'We don't really know. As the new owners of Gulabrai Villa we welcome you all to our house-warming breakfast. Would you like some pakwaan daal?'

The Gulabrais and Benjamin had made their escape. They were in Benjamin's private yacht which had left Karachi port in the wee hours of the morning. While Karachi speculated, cursed and ranted, they were fast asleep in their respective cabins as the yacht sailed across a calm Arabian Sea. There was little the fair citizens of Karachi could do.

There was little too, that Sati could do as she watched the sun setting into the Arabian Sea later that evening. When her father asked her what was wrong, she snapped at him. Benjamin approached her tentatively with a drink and was told to chuck it into the sea. She paced up and down the not very large deck. Here she was in the wide-open sea, feeling claustrophobic.

Finally, at dinner that night, she confronted both of them. 'Here's to the smoothest exit ever,' she said raising her glass of nimbu pani, as they raised their wine glasses. 'But we have a small, unanticipated bump on the way.'

'First', her father said, 'I want to congratulate the two of you on the fantastic charade you carried out. While everyone in Karachi was talking about you, their attention was diverted from what Benjamin and I were up to. Sayyed, who had had his eyes on our house for a long time, and was trying to buy it at a much lower price, came close to guessing that something was up, but his long patrician nose couldn't sniff out the facts. Thank you, both of you. Cheers to the future.'

Sati was silent. Benjamin and her father were in great spirits. Should she mention the bump or let it pass? At times like these she missed her mother more than ever.

'What's this bump you were talking about?' her father asked.

Benjamin, who knew exactly what she was talking about, quietly choked on his drink.

'What all of us failed to include in our calculations was the minor matter of me,' she said trying to be business-like, but in fact on the verge of tears. 'I'm in love and don't know what to do about it.'

'With whom?' Vishnu asked. 'The only person you've been with is Benjamin and ...' As realization dawned, he looked stricken. 'Don't be ridiculous. Benjamin? You're in love with Benjamin?'

The strain, the tension of the last few weeks finally got to him. He was having a heart attack.

'Mr Gulabrai, I was just playing a part. I swear on the Torah ...'

'Oh Benjamin, my young friend Ben ... ja ... min. You ... played your part too well. Oh hell ... Take ... care ... of her.'

And he collapsed. Purple in the face. No heartbeat, no pulse. Just like that. Gone. In the middle of the sea. The doctor on board couldn't help. But even a cardiac specialist couldn't have helped. Vishnu had dissembled well. No one knew of his heart problems except for Benjamin, and he had been sworn to secrecy.

Sati was quiet. And calm. She walked into her cabin, rummaged around in her trunk, came out with her Kodak Vigilant and started snapping pictures of the sea around the yacht, the crew, Benjamin, seagulls, flying fish. She went through roll after roll after roll in a cold frenzy. Not one picture of her dead father.

'I didn't want one,' Sati G said softly as she recalled that day. 'For a very long time, I blamed myself for his death. If I'd kept quiet about my feelings, would he still be alive? I *had* to – I *wanted* to – remember him alive,' Sati G told me. 'I have them framed and mounted in my study at home. A series of large photographs in a series called The Last Journey.'

'The body has been stowed away, Mr Zachariah.'

'What's the protocol, Captain Jones?'

'Burial at sea or head to the nearest port, Bombay.'

'Bombay, I think.'

Sati, who was still busy taking photographs, shook her head.

'Burial at sea,' she said in her unnaturally calm voice, took a picture and moved away, still clicking.

All the way to Ceylon, through the Palk Straits, and up the east coast of India, she clicked. She clicked long after her film rolls had run out, and was still clicking when the yacht sailed into Calcutta and moored at one of the docks in Kidderpore.

Other than some perfunctory good mornings and 'pass the salt please' exchanges, very little was said on the long voyage. They moved into his apartment at Queen's Mansion, Park Street, in Calcutta, and they had separate rooms.

It was a sprawling apartment spread out over six bedrooms, a dining room, a living room and even an ante-room. Tastefully decorated, but definitely a man's home. No woman had ever been here, that much was obvious to Sati.

They still hadn't exchanged a word. Both of them were grieving. She for her father and Benjamin for the best friend he had ever had.

Weeks went by. Benjamin took her on a social whirl around the city. She met everybody, but never said more than 'hello' to all the people she met. They thought she was a snob. It didn't matter. She never met the same person twice.

But she was listening to what they were saying, to what they enjoyed, to their thoughts. And, even though she didn't know it then, a germ of an idea was taking shape in her troubled mind.

He came out of his bedroom late one evening, immaculately dressed. She was in the balcony that overlooked Park Street. He came and stood by her. He had a thick folder with him. They watched the Victorias trot past with slightly worried memsaabs in them. They saw the occasional automobile driven by a local, hooting its way down the street.

'I made a promise to your father that I would take care of you, and I intend to keep that promise.' he said.

'What's in that folder?' she asked, not concealing the bitterness she felt. 'My late father's wealth?'

'No. This arrived from Karachi yesterday. Why don't you take a look?'

She opened the folder and went through its contents, reading each page slowly, absorbing all that each page said. She looked bewildered.

Benjamin looked at her. 'He didn't have much of a heart left to begin with. He had high BP, and I guess all those things caught up with him. So you don't need to blame yourself for his death.'

'And now it's just you and me.'

'I'll be here as long as you need me.'

There was a long silence. And, for the first time in a long while, she looked into his eyes. 'But you don't love me. Yes?'

'I can't. Not the way you want me to.'

'You were very convincing in Karachi.'

'I had to be. We'd never have escaped otherwise.'

'But we are still married?'

'Officially, legally, on paper, yes.'

He was about to say something and stopped. He looked at her trying to gauge if she would understand, if she would accept him for what he was. They settled down under the awning in the balcony. He poured a drink for himself, took a sip, still struggling. He took her hands in his and looked into her eyes, willing her to understand. 'Sati, I am a homosexual.'

He waited for shock, horror, anger, disgust. But all she did was look at him, enquiringly. 'Benjamin, what's a homosexual?'

She laughed. How she laughed that day, sitting in the car! The whole car shook with her laughter.

'You should have seen his face.' Still giggling helplessly, she rummaged around in her bag with her diamond laden fingers, took out a gold cigarette case and a diamond-dust lighter, and lit her cigarette. I rolled the window down discreetly. 'What dear Benjamin hadn't known was that when he promised my father he'd take care of me, he'd have to help me grow up in every way. All I knew about sex was what my mother had told me when she was alive. "It will hurt the first time and, if you're lucky, it will get better."'

Benjamin was the perfect guide, mentor and friend. The world at large thought they were the ideal couple. And not just the small world that was Calcutta. He took her around the country, making sure that Khajuraho was on the itinerary. He took her on his business trips abroad. She was a quick learner.

1948. In Lebanon, still in the euphoria of newly found freedom from the shackles of the French – the Lebanese had got their independence a year before India did. Sitting at a night club, Sati decided what she wanted to do with her life.

'How much am I worth?' she asked Benjamin.

'In Sterling a million, give or take a few hundred thousand.'

'I didn't know Baba was so wealthy.'

'It's a decent amount,' he acknowledged, smiling.

'Calcutta is boring. We need a place like this there. Do I have enough to set up a place like this there?'

A week later they were back in Calcutta. Frenzied activity followed, rushing from one place to another, getting the necessary permissions, identifying the place, buying it. Palms were greased and, where that didn't work, Sati's infinite charm smoothed the way.

'What do we call the place?'

They fought about that. He wanted to call it Sati G's. She wanted an English-sounding name. She felt that would be more effective. As a name, Benji's was too soft. So she fought for Zack's. And got it. It was a winner from day one.

Decorators were imported from Paris, recipes from all round the world; women from Lebanon to act as hostesses. There was liquor of all kinds, with sommeliers from France to advise you on your selection of wines. At one time there were at least a dozen foreign languages being spoken in those twenty thousand square feet of space as it transformed itself from a rundown warehouse to Zack's.

Opening night was by invitation only. Everybody who was anybody was there. Anybody who wasn't was deeply annoyed.

Firpo's at the Great Eastern Hotel looked like a drab old aunt in comparison. Ferrazini's on Chowringhee Road was yesterday's news. And Sati was finally home. Benjamin was the front man. Everybody over a period of time suspected that she owned the place, but no one was too sure.

Once the customers, especially shop owners of the New Market, discovered that the Lebanese hostesses served more than just food and drink, they were there every evening. Business was booming and for fifteen years it ran smoothly.

But all it takes is a disgruntled wife who has got it in for her husband to cause a slide. One such started a smear campaign. And it spread.

'I won't tell you who it was, but she was one of the cats of the SLA.'

Sati G got a phone call one morning from Lalbazaar Police Station. It was the commissioner's PA. He asked her not to be present at Zack's that night.

There was a raid. Everything was above board. The police discovered nothing. The press covered that raid. They said a few nasty things about the place. But by and large they gave it a clean chit.

She had won. And the disgruntled wife never forgave her. She told the cat's husband to stop coming. He was disappointed, but he understood.

Much mud had been slung at the club and at her reputation. Some of it stuck in spite of Benjamin doing a superb whitewash job. They lost a few friends in high places though. She was now called a brothel keeper.

'So I decided I would be one. I organized all the women and gave them a code of conduct which they followed to the letter. That kept them out of trouble.'

Though completely illegal, her houses were the best-kept houses in Calcutta. She told an MLA friend that if the government legalized the business, they could earn a fortune in taxes. He wasn't amused.

Benjamin and she came to love each other over a period of time. But they never shared a bedroom. He had a favourite Lebanese boy, the brother of one of the girls. He would visit once a week. Sati enjoyed sex very much. And had a similar arrangement. Benjamin walked in on them one evening and was horrified to learn that his special boy was hers too.

'We had a good laugh about it later. It brought us closer. And, young man, you needn't ask the next question. The answer is no. The three of us never did it together.'

She was devastated when Benjamin decided he wanted to settle down in Israel. 'I've been a wanderer all my life. I want a home,' he said.

He had done more for her than any other human being ever had. She couldn't stand in his way. Wouldn't. She took over the running of the place. Her friends in high places left or were transferred out one by one. Their replacements never could understand how Zack's functioned. And soon they became greedy. In the past, it was favour for favour and the administration and Benjamin got on fine. Now it was under the table payments, which became impossible to sustain over time. She could see her clientele drifting away and being replaced by the dregs. But the dregs had the money. The underworld, crooked politicians, purveyors of sleaze.

'It's no fun anymore.'

She looked out of the car window at the mist.

'When you look at me, you see a slightly notorious and fashionable lady dressed in pink. When I look in the mirror, I see a bored woman. One day I'll just take away all of it and disappear. It will be as if Zack's never existed; Sati G never existed.'

We sat silently in the car, by the river, looking at a ship being piloted out to sea, until it disappeared into the mist that had become heavier over the Hooghly.

'That's all you are getting from me. Time to drop you home.'

And she did. I stood at our gate watching her car drive away into the Calcutta smog.

'Notorious Nightclub Shuts Down' screamed a banner headline a few years later, on a Monday morning. A brief description followed, of the goings on in Zack's, about its shady owner, sailors et cetera, ending with a holier-than-thou line about how the neighbourhood could only be a better place now.

On Wednesday a small announcement in the Personal Column, under Deaths, of the same paper, said:

Zachariah Sati: Saturday, August 3, of natural causes. At her request, no flowers, no wreaths, no memorial meetings. Cremated on Sunday, August 4.

That was that. I walked to Zack's that Wednesday morning. The doors were wide open. The place was desolate and bare. All the trappings had been removed. Just one chandelier was left on the floor waiting to be packed. I never knew where she lived and it seemed nobody did. She had been right. She had taken it all away and disappeared.

Free School Street would never be the same again on Saturday nights.

One Sunday morning, a few months later I walked into Flury's with a friend, a doctor, in fact the family doctor to the Zachariah's.

We walked up to a frail old man sipping a cup of coffee and nibbling on a Diplomat – a frothy creamy concoction soaked in rum.

'And who is this young man?' he asked my friend.

My friend introduced us. This was the famous Benjamin Zachariah, Sati G's husband.

'Your wife, Sati Aunty, and I went on a long drive once and she told me her story.'

'Of course, you're the one with the "holy mother"? She told me about you. Did she tell you that Diplomats were absolutely her all-time favourite?'

'No,' I replied.

'Ah! There is a lot she didn't tell you. If ever you tell her story, be kind.'

And he went back to nibbling his Diplomat.

A few days later, a large crate landed up at our doorstep addressed to me, accompanied with a card. We opened the crate and unpacked about thirty large 40x30 prints taken on a format I'd never seen. We laid them out on the grass in the garden.

They were exquisite, slightly browned by age. Portraits at sea. Sailors at work; a handsome man staring into the distance

(Benjamin?); the captain in the dim light of the night looking at his charts; flying fish keeping pace with the yacht; a black and white sunset. The technique, framing, light would have made Bresson proud.

The last one was a shot of six sailors in a lifeboat, the sun setting behind them, saluting as the last few inches of a coffin made its way to its final resting place. It was the only one that was blurred – as though her hands had trembled when she took it.

Anustup and Mamlu

He strolled into the New Kenilworth Hotel in Little Russell Street as he did every day in December, on the dot at noon, with all the Bengali and English newspapers that had been delivered to him. Though he had made no formal reservation, they always kept a chair for him in the garden under a red-and-white striped umbrella. He was a regular.

Winter afternoons in Calcutta were pleasant, and he had been coming here for the last few years. He always ordered chilli 'frog legs.' The waiters found it amusing that he called their boneless chilli chicken 'frog legs.'

'What can I do?' he said. 'They taste just like the frog legs I used to have in Paris.'

He was about forty-five years old, a gentleman of the old school, John Lennon glasses perched precariously on the tip of his slightly hooked nose. He had a broad forehead over bright, inquisitive eyes, across which ran one black eyebrow, as if the Almighty had dipped his thumb in surma and run it across all the way from left to right in one stroke. On top of this was a mane of prematurely white hair.

By the time he had settled down on his chair, a bottle of chilled Sunlager would arrive. The waiter, who knew exactly how he liked it, would tilt the glass just so, and pour out the amber liquid very slowly so that Anustup always got just a quarter-inch of head. He would smile appreciatively, thank the waiter, and take his first sip. By the time he'd finished the first glass and his first newspaper, his 'frog legs' would've arrived, and the waiter would pour out the second glass.

Today, he just gulped the first glass down and stared at a white envelope he'd placed on the table, terrified, his waiter and his newspaper both ignored for the moment.

Three months ago, a friend of his who had come back to India for a holiday from Saudi Arabia had suggested that he apply for a professorial vacancy in that country.

'Dhoor sala,' he'd said contemptuously. 'I don't want to go to some Arab country to teach in a business school.'

'Don't be such a tight-assed bokachoda. If, and there is no guarantee you will get the job, you do get it, work for two years, bank your salary, and you will never have to work again.'

'How long have you been working there? Six years now?'

'My case is different. I have four children I have to put through college. And not one of them is intelligent enough to qualify for a scholarship. You and Mamlu have no kids and don't want any. Two years in Saudi, and you will be set up for life.'

'What about Mamlu's job?'

'Come on, Stup, your wife is a consultant with the UNDP and she spends most of the time in sub-Saharan Africa trying to tackle the AIDS pandemic. Instead of coming home to Calcutta, she'll go home to Riyadh.'

Anustup thought about it for a few days and, after some rare consultation with his wife Mamlu, (he very rarely consulted her about anything), they both came to the conclusion that it wouldn't be such a bad idea after all.

Much correspondence and many interviews later, he got a confirmation letter. The job was his and all that was left was the formality of a medical examination. Could he present himself at the Wellesley Medical Centre for the necessary tests? After being poked, probed, and prodded by a host of pathologists and lab technicians, he left behind 'a bloody armful of blood' as he told his friend that evening after a few drinks. Then he waited for the results.

On getting home that evening, not exactly sober (Mamlu was on tour so he'd had the extra two or was it three?), he was glancing idly through the list of tests the lab was going to do.

The name of one test leapt out at him.

ELISA.

His hands shook.

A few years ago, he had been on the advisory board of a government agency that had been negotiating an IMF loan. On the streets of Calcutta in those days, the IMF was commonly known as the International Mother Fucker. And the joke doing the rounds was that the only difference between the IMF and HIV was that the IMF first gave you AIDS and then it screwed you.

The average age of the IMF delegation that arrived was around thirty. The leader of the delegation was a lady called Susan. For a middle class, sexually repressed, third-world male as Anustup described himself, Susan was a walking-talking sexual fantasy.

All through the many presentations, slides, charts, facts and figures, he became pretty certain that was all she would ever be – a fantasy.

Susan was a hard-headed negotiator. So was Anustup.

The thrust, parry, counter thrust, the feint at the negotiating table, were just the opening moves. Foreplay at its best. And it came as no surprise to anyone at the table, except to Anustup, that he and Susan ended up in bed that night. It was the most fantastic sex he'd ever had. Senseless, mad, energetic sex.

He was not one of those men who would rush to the nearest bar immediately afterwards and boast about his conquest to his colleagues and friends. He might have liked to talk about the experience with a very good friend. But in this world he had only one. And he was married to her. He could hardly talk to her about it

Until he'd read the word 'ELISA', Susan had been a pleasant memory, someone he'd thought of now and then. He distinctly remembered *not* using a condom.

He stared at the white envelope. It contained the pathology tests results. He had two empty bottles of beer on the table. He didn't remember drinking them. The 'frog legs' had turned cold.

The waiters hovered around, looking worried. A middle-aged gentleman, who was also a regular and regularly scrounged a cigarette off Anustup, walked hesitantly up to his table.

'Sair, can I borrow a cigarette?'

In normal circumstances, Anustup would have pushed his packet forward on the table. The borrower would have taken a cigarette out, lit it, taken a deep satisfying drag, said thank you, and moved back to his table.

Not today. Anustup was looking for an excuse, any excuse, to postpone opening the envelope.

'Borrow! Borrow a cigarette! What are you going to do after you've smoked it? Return the ashes to me?'

The man stood there in a state of shock. He had never heard Anustup's loud baritone before. And he certainly had not imagined that a mild-mannered bhadralok could be so rude. No one in the hotel ever had, and they all turned – staff and fellow patrons, and looked at Anustup in surprise and bewilderment.

No one was more surprised at this behaviour than Anustup himself. 'What on earth is wrong with me?' he thought. 'Maybe if I talked to a stranger, I could get over this … this fear of the envelope.'

'I'll lend you a cigarette if you'll sit down and talk.'

'Why should I?' the now-belligerent man replied.

'Because I need to talk to someone.'

'Farst you are being rude, then you want to chatter with me. You are a nonsense and a sinister. I will parchase my own cigarette,' he said loudly as he walked away from Anustup's table. On any other day, Anustup would have quietly smiled at the man's peculiar use of the English language. Never before in his life, had he been called either 'a nonsense' or 'a sinister.' But not today.

Today, Anustup looked around the restaurant. His eyes moved from table to table. The other patrons looked away, mildly upset that they had been caught eavesdropping. He played with the envelope for a bit. Should he or shouldn't he open it?

He didn't.

He picked up one of his newspapers and hid himself behind it.

It's amazing how, when you wish to forget something, the whole world conspires to make sure that you don't. Every page he turned to in the newspaper had at least two or more articles on HIV/AIDS.

One article, albeit a small one, reported a rape of a thirty-four-year-old woman at a fire station.

She said she had gone to Bhawanipur Fire Station to meet with one of the firefighters whom she had met when there had been a false alarm in the bustee where she lived. One thing led to another, and they were in the throes of sex when the others joined in the romp.

This got Anustup thinking.

If it was a premeditated 'romp', then the rapists should get what was coming to them, several years in jail or hanging by their dicks, or whatever the justice system deemed a fit punishment. But if they walked in on the scene and decided to join in the 'romp' on the *sperm* of the moment, then they were in bigger trouble. Obviously there weren't going to be enough condoms going around if there were any at all, so being hanged by their dicks would be the least of their problems.

Anustup tried to recreate the scenario. On one side you had the thirty-four-year-old woman and a firefighter had decided to have it off. On the other you had the 'rompers' who walked in on the scene and were riveted by the action. And they decided to join in against the woman's will. If the original couple knew what they were getting into, they must have carried condoms with them. But what about the other 'rompers'? Let's call them by their real name, he thought. *Rapists*. Did rapists carry around condoms? ('Just hold still, madam. I have to put this on before I rape you.')

Somehow Anustup didn't think so.

So you had a total of five people exchanging bodily fluids. And if it was rape, there was bound to be a certain amount of violence. As sure as hell, a condom was going to tear or a diaphragm going to shift.

If even one of them, unknowingly, was HIV-positive, there was a likelihood that the virus now had five more warm homes to set ablaze. And these would be fires that no fire station could put out.

As much as he tried to avoid thinking about it, he couldn't. HIV/AIDS and that damned envelope kept intruding into his thoughts. He swept the newspapers to the ground and placed the envelope at the centre of the table.

He noticed that he was down to his last cigarette. Should he smoke it before or after opening the envelope? Should he open it at all?

Most of the envelopes or letters he'd ever opened in his life had been disappointing, to say the least. He remembered the time he was a student in England doing his actuaries. He used to receive an aerogramme nearly every week from his father. It was usually a status report on what the family was up to or had been up to in the preceding week, and usually ended with an admonishing note at the end about Anustup's lack of correspondence. Though boring, in its way the letter was also oddly reassuring for a young man on his own in England.

However, there was a time when he received a hand-delivered (not mailed) envelope from home that left him devastated. It had his father's handwriting on the envelope. Inside was a short note from his father:

Dear Anu
Enclosed are fifty pounds which I have asked your chhoto kaku to carry for you. Spend them well. Write more often.
Tomar,
Baba

Stapled to the letter were some rather unpleasant looking pound notes of various denominations that had seen better days. But Anustup wasn't complaining.

There was another short letter from his elder brother in the same envelope.

Dear Stup,
Baba had a stroke and died a few days ago. His last words were, 'Tell Anu to finish his studies and return.'
Tai karo.
Tomar,
Barda

He had cried for weeks afterwards.

There was another envelope he remembered from a company called Guest, Keen and Williams – a large engineering company that had its factory on the west side of the Hooghly. After a very successful interview, he'd been assured the job of additional secretary was his. The letter that arrived in an official-looking envelope was a glowing tribute to his qualifications. However, 'it was with deep regret' they informed him that 'because of circumstances beyond the control of the company' at that time, it was not possible for them to offer him the position.

The beers had long since given way to pink gins. He found a few empty glasses on his table. He needed to go to the loo. He'd open the damned envelope afterwards.

While washing his hands he looked at his bloodshot eyes in the mirror. He was very drunk. And he thought of the letter he'd written to the first woman he'd ever been in love with. With great care he had penned a twelve-page epistle to her – an ode to her beauty, professing his undying love for her. He remembered her reply too. The next morning he had opened an envelope from her with a note that said 'Piss off. Grow up.'

He felt a wave of self-pity as a single tear rolled down his cheek, self-pity of a kind that only a drunk could empathize with.

He didn't return to his table.

An hour or so later, a waiter cleared it. 'Sir,' he said to the manager, 'Anustup Babu has left this behind,' and handed him the unopened envelope. 'He has not settled his bill either.'

'Hmm, he was upset about something. Don't worry. He'll be back tomorrow. We'll keep it for him.'

Everybody makes a big deal about HIV. As they should. But like every other thing, HIV can be managed. It can be handled. Anustup and I talked about it. But face-to-face? Never. That's not the way he does things. In all the years I have known him, lived with him, loved him, he has never confronted me with an issue. He hates confrontation. He loves procrastination. Procrastination, he would say, is the mother of all inventions.

Let me give you an example. In the days of landline telephones, a major instrument in our lives because we both travelled to various places for our work, he'd telephone. I mean, we'd have spent weeks together living in the same old house in Ballygunge, and wouldn't have exchanged a word about anything important. But the minute he went off travelling, he'd phone to tell me about an aunt (very dear to us) who had developed cancer or a sister who's been admitted to the hospital for surgery.

'When was this?'

'Oh … about a week ago.'

'Why didn't you mention it a week ago? When you were here?'

'Oh you know …' His voice would trail away into silence,

Now, I am not a violent person, but at moments like this I could cheerfully throttle him. But he wasn't there, was he? In these days of emails, he's better off than he ever was before. He doesn't have to confront anybody or anything either face-to-face or by phone. He writes – long rambling letters that somewhere in the middle, mention in passing, what the letter is really all about.

And it took him about four emails to write about his latest predicament. But, as I said, HIV can be handled. It isn't the end of the world. It can be managed.

To understand what happened between Anustup, my husband, and me, I need to tell you about Anubha.

Anubha was a petite young thing who studied engineering at Jadavpur University.

I used to be in the Arts College at the same university. We met in the coffee house close to the campus and, within minutes, became lifelong friends.

She is now a big, beautiful lady, with her feet firmly planted in reality. She has a double doctorate, has written white papers on various subjects, and is respected worldwide as an erudite scholar. About a year ago on her way home one night, she was raped. Later, she discovered that she had contracted the AIDS virus.

'At first,' she said, 'I was angry. I was in such a rage. I wanted to track down the man with all the resources that I could muster, and have him killed. Not because he'd raped me but because he'd sentenced me to death.'

A few months later the rage had left her.

'HIV-positive or not, we're all sentenced to die anyway. My death will come a bit sooner than I thought it would. I've lived my life and, though a bit differently now, I am still living it.'

During her travels she'd met babies who were HIV-positive, babies who would never know the joy of living.

'"So grow up, girl," I told myself,' she said. 'I've met PLWHA – People Living With HIV/AIDS – on their last legs, who can't afford medication. I've met families ravaged by the virus, who have nothing to look forward to except a slow, painful death. *So grow up, girl*, I tell myself. Start living again.'

'The anger has never left me, but mind-destroying rage has. I am still angry with the man who did this to me. But I *do* want to meet him. If ever I see him, I will know him. I'll walk up to him and introduce myself and tell him what he's done to me. And then I will tell him that I forgive him.'

And then, as if she was rehearsing the line, or had said it many times in her head, she said with the gentlest expression on her face, 'I forgive you for raping me. I forgive you for giving making me a PLWHA. But I shall not forgive you for stealing my identity. Not now, not yet.'

At an international conference on PLWHA at the Grand Hotel in Calcutta, Anubha and I stood at the entrance of the room welcoming delegates from four or five countries with a warm handshake. We took our places around a round table. As we all were strangers to each other, we had to get up one by one, introduce ourselves, and say a sentence about ourselves.

'I'm George. I'm an actor.'

'I'm Penelope, and I love the colour blue.'

'I'm Georgina. (Giggle) Hi, George. And I hate dusk.'

'I'm Ketaki, and I hate the fuss made about something as ordinary as *chicken tikka*.'

'Hi, I'm Anubha. And I am HIV-positive.'

Silence. Followed by the rest of the stuttered introductions no one heard.

Anubha sat through them with a sad smile on her face. She knew, though no one looked directly at her, that she was being scrutinized from the corners of their eyes, through her reflection on a window opposite.

One set of hands disappeared under the table, and began wiping themselves furiously with the table cloth.

Penelope, almost absent-mindedly, used her handkerchief (a blue one, I might add) to wipe her palm. She realized what she was doing, stopped, started putting it away in her purse, looked at it suspiciously, and 'accidentally' dropped it on the floor.

And George? He had the funniest reaction. He took a sip of water and, as realization dawned, choked, looked at his offensive right hand, wiped it, took a sip with his left and choked again. He hurriedly put down the glass which had been touched by his right hand and glared at it. He never took his eyes off the glass until the round of introductions was over. If there had been two more introductions to go through, the glass would have shattered – such was the intensity of his gaze.

Anubha took the floor. 'Ladies and gentlemen, welcome to the Transformation through Arts and Media workshop on HIV/AIDS. I can assure you that you cannot get AIDS through shaking hands. Obviously, no one in this room has read all the pre-workshop literature that was sent to them. That is par for the course.'

Nervous laughs around the table.

Except for George, who still glared fixedly – not at the glass, but at Anubha.

Nervous comments began. 'Oh, so this was a test ...' 'So you're not er ... um ...' 'Anubha how could you ...?' 'Oh, this was some sort of test ...'

'No, it was not a test. And yes, I have tested positive for HIV.'

Over the years I learnt a lot from her, and I hope she learnt a little from me. We shared rooms wherever we met and shared our fears, dreams, and hopes.

Once, after a rather harrowing trip to Bangkok, we landed in Calcutta around three in the morning. The airport was in its usual chaotic state. Touts of every shape and colour approached us.

'Do we look like we don't belong?' I asked Anubha. We tried to ignore them, but were slowly being cornered. One of them accidentally touched me, while trying to hand me a flyer for a cheap, seedy hotel. Anubha noticed this and, very sweetly, with a smile on her face, said, 'Ai. Bokachoda, tomar ma nei, bon nei, aamadeyer gai haath keno deechchho?' (Hey, dumbfuck, don't you have a mother or sister, why are you pawing us?)

They were stunned into inaction, and quietly melted away.

Her car arrived. We got into it. On our way to my house, she asked her driver to stop at the Victoria Memorial. I was a bit puzzled. It was late. I was tired and needed a shower.

'Just a few minutes,' she said.

We got off the car, and sat on the steps of the statue of Queen Victoria. She looked at the Calcutta Maidan stretched out in front of her. The first rays of the sun had started making their presence felt.

She shuddered.

'I'd come out for a morning walk exactly at this time. There wasn't a soul in sight. I sat here, exactly where we are sitting. I was mugged and raped. Right here.'

I didn't say anything. It was slowly becoming brighter. In the distance a herd of goats were feeding on the Maidan grass. A few early morning walkers were making their appearance.

'You can handle rape. You can handle HIV too. Your first instincts are rage, anger, hate. *Why me?* Life is unfair. If I've got it, well, I'm not going to live with it alone. If life is unfair to me, it can be so to someone else. So I'll spread it, and to hell with the consequences. No amount of education, no doctorates, no white papers, nothing is relevant anymore.'

She paused.

'And then you learn to control it. Slowly. You start looking at yourself. And you learn to handle it.'

It was frightening, what she told me ... Did she? ... Could she have spread it around in her rage? I didn't want to know.

'Today, all I am is Anubha Basu, PLWHA. And that's all that matters to everyone now. So I can forgive that man for raping me. I can forgive him for making me a PLWHA. But I cannot forgive him for stealing from me what I am, for destroying my identity as everything but an HIV patient. No, I cannot be that noble. That will require someone of far more strength and nobility to be able to do that.'

But Anubha gives me strength. Knowing all that she's been through, and is still going through, I can handle it too.

Anustup's email was a rambling one in which, somewhere, tucked away in the middle of a series of trivialities, he confessed his indiscretion of a few years ago. His new job required him to be tested for HIV. And he was sitting in Calcutta, unable to slit open the envelope that had his report.

Confusion. Anger. Rage. I began to understand what Anubha must have felt. Not anywhere near hers I'm sure, but it was there. There was not a moment to waste. I rushed to the pathology lab and had my blood tested.

I waited for the report.

Negative.

I am not a PLWHA.

I have, over the years, met a number of people who are living with HIV/AIDS and, though I am comfortable working with them, or living with them, the sense of relief when the results arrived was overwhelming. For the last thirteen years I have lived with a man, not knowing that he betrayed the trust we had built our togetherness on. Supposing he had contracted the virus and passed it on to me?

We could have done something about it. Perhaps.

Together, perhaps – thanks to Anubha, and the years I've spent attending and conducting workshops around the world dealing with and learning about People Living With HIV/AIDS.

But betrayal? I can't handle that.

I don't know how. I never attended any workshops on betrayal.

Anila

*M*y *Dearest,*

You have often told me that you will never leave Calcutta. And I have no intentions of staying here any longer.

But first, before you blame yourself, let me tell you I am not leaving because of the situation we are in. We have had four great years together. Our affair began because I was miserable living with my husband. You rescued me from the claustrophobia of it all.

Thank you so much for introducing me to a side of Calcutta I never knew existed. 'Calcutta 16' as you called it and as it was. Through the people I met in Free School Street, the New Market, Sudder Street and Chowringhee Lane where you lived; through you and through their stories that you told me. Of success, of failure. Of philanthropy, of prostitution. Of dope peddlers with a heart of gold. Of peddlers who will maim and murder at the drop of a chillum. Of refugees who came across the borders and made their fortunes. Of down to earth, real people who made your world and who I didn't know existed because I was born, brought up, and married in the rarefied atmosphere of Old Alipur. Just four miles away. Another world, another planet.

But it is time to leave my husband for good. It is time to leave Calcutta and, alas, it is time to leave you.

My husband, who was well aware of what was going on between you and me, and chose to ignore it, is now livid at my leaving.

'What will people say?' he screamed.

'How can you do this to me?'

How 'can' I do this to him? That is indeed a question that needs an answer.

So I wrote a little fairy tale.

Think of it as a piece of whimsy which I can share only with you, my darling, since you're the one who brought 'music' into my life and gave it a sense of playfulness it never had.

Think of this as a farewell present. And if and when you miss me, read it and remember me.

Think of it as a long shaggy dog story which you with your weird sense of the ridiculous would appreciate.

Think of it too, as a tribute to all those wonderfully real people amongst whom you live, who in spite of all their troubles taught me how to laugh, not just at the vagaries of life but at myself.

(Some of the descriptions are quotes from you, which I realized later were quotes from the Kama Sutra, you bastard!)

In the land of Artha there once lived a king in a palace so beautiful that people, both commoners and those of royal blood, came to view its grandeur.

The king himself was old and wise. He had fought many battles, won a few, and lost some. And his life had been lived to the full.

Until now.

As he sat on his throne, he looked out at the world with a tinge of regret. His queen of two score years or so enquired gently what was bothering him.

'I have everything a king could want. I have conquered lands; I have riches beyond belief; I have subjects who are content; I have you, my wife, who has stood by me through all the troubled times and the good. Citizens of the world come to pay their respects to my kingdom but, more importantly, they come to hear my music. Music that has been passed down from generation to generation in this royal house. But what has it all been for? I have a young prince ready to don my mantle after I pass. But I have no heir to continue the music that has made this kingdom so famous.'

'Maharaj, your youngest son, Ganesha, has been trained in all the nuances of your gharana and will continue the glorious tradition,' his vazir pointed out.

'Our youngest son was named after the elephant god. Unfortunately, he sounds much like an elephant and very little like a god.'

His queen intervened. 'Maharaj, you are too cruel. He has the voice of an angel, and as it soars through the palace, all the courtiers stop to listen in wonder.'

'In wonder indeed,' continued the king. 'In wonder that a king so well versed in music should produce such a tuneless heir.'

The courtiers chuckled appreciatively at the intended pun.

'The play on words was not *that* humourous,' he said. 'My son has the skill, he has the voice, and he has the knowledge, but his singing lacks that one ingredient which would make it great. It lacks heart.'

Somewhere else in the palace, the prince, a handsome young man of some sixteen years, sits at a tanpura surrounded by women who hang on to every note he sings. What are the women there for? To hear him sing? No. They are simply there to admire his beauty. Each is coquettish in her own way. But he is oblivious to them as he sings.

Behind him sits his guru – a plump, genial old man who, if he had any hair, would pull at it in frustration. Because as the king said, the prince has everything. Except heart.

The guru claps his hands. The music stops. The prince looks puzzled. The ladies leave the room, some disappointed, some arranging liaisons with each other, some whispering to the eunuch nearby as they leave the room in various states of disarray hoping that the prince will catch a glimpse of them ... but no. The prince just looks at his guru, still puzzled.

'Go, go,' says the guru. 'Go to your archery classes or whatever it is you young men do.'

'But guruji, what about my riyaaz?'

'You, Your Royal Highness, are an ant. Like an ant, you are meticulous, precise and proper. You will always build the perfect anthill with your song. But that is all it will ever be. It will never be a palace of music. Just an anthill.'

The prince leaves the room, not particularly dejected since he thinks he has just been paid a compliment.

Guruji's wife enters. She is a woman so exquisite that one wonders how someone as plump and unattractive as guruji could have got her for a wife.

'Surely, you were a bit rash in describing the prince as an ant. Princes can be temperamental and, one fine day, he'll have this perfect round head of yours served to him on a platter of gold because you insulted him.'

'That is the day I will look forward to. At least I will not have to subject myself again to his caterwauling.'

'Who then will take care of this,' his wife says, as she lets her chemise fall. Her husband stares as the glorious figure, and her eyes looking at him coquettishly – eager, inviting.

'Ah. All the music in the world is nothing compared to you,' says guruji. 'A king would travel across continents to win your body. Your hair as black as kohl. Your eyes as dark and pure. Your cheeks a perfect oval; your nose excels in elegance, your mouth … waiting to be kissed, enhances the vermillon of both your lips and tongue, your neck stretched in poise – a gazelle would hide its own in embarrassment …' he continues, quoting from some esoteric erotic verse he had read the previous evening.

And he extols all her virtues and physical attributes in a song. And, as the song continues, they retire to bed where, behind a lace curtain, he makes love to her most beautifully.

Meanwhile, the prince walks to the courtyard where an archery lesson is in progress. He is welcomed by all his fellow students and courtiers who bow to him.

'Over here, I am not your prince. I am but a subject of the great archer, who has so kindly decided to impart all his skills and knowledge to us. Oh Acharya, if we learn but one tenth of what you have, we will be able to show off our skills to all the world and make you proud. We bow to you and your skills.'

And they do. The lessons begin. The prince isn't much good at archery either. But the windows that overlook the courtyard have a number of women of all ages and sizes who swoon at the prince's beauty. Every time he lifts the bow, they sigh. Every time he pulls the string, they look lasciviously at his rippling muscles and wonder quite audibly about his arrow and the direction it will take. The prince approaches one of his fellow students and asks him how he can improve his shooting skills. The friend, who is bit of a rake, compares archery to the body of a woman.

'The curve of the bow is like the calf of a virginal girl. The string must be pulled just so, so that all the knowledge it shrouds is revealed at one go, and the target is there in all its splendour waiting to be pierced by the arrow.'

The prince looks at his friend as if the latter has lost his mind. He picks up his bow and arrow, and shoots. It misses the target by about a mile, and all his friends burst out laughing.

Guruji and his wife, Priamvade, are in bed, satiated for the moment. Slowly, the wife's thoughts drift to her worried-looking husband, and she speaks up after a pause.

'My lord, do you not realize what is wrong with the prince? He is but a child and doesn't know about the pleasures that await him.'

'Priamvade, my wife, my horn of plenty, why don't you speak in a language we mere mortals understand?'

'My lord, the prince will never understand the art of music until he has enjoyed the pleasures a woman can offer him. Perhaps then he ...'

'Do you mean to say, my divine love, that the prince is a virgin?'

'That is exactly what I mean and, if my lord will permit, I can arrange for him to be exposed to all the wonders of growing into manhood. Step by seductive step.'

'This is indeed a major decision and cannot be taken without the consent of the king.'

'More than just being the master musician in this palace, you are his friend. You have been at his side for over a quarter of a century. I am sure that he will listen to your advice if you offer it.'

'I shall go immediately, and apprise His Majesty of your thoughts.'

'Maharaj, His Majesty will now be in the royal baths. We have an hour or so to ourselves. Do you have the strength to attempt the Vyanta Bandha?'

So saying she turns around, lies on her stomach, and looks longingly at guruji.

Meanwhile in the royal baths, the king is being cared for by his courtiers. At one end of the bath, a sitar player gently plays a raga. A handmaiden enters the bath and the king stands up. She folds him in a large drying cloth, and gently leads him out of the bath and onto an ornate chair near the queen. The king and queen talk about the prince and wonder what they should do.

'Surely, there must be one wise man in our kingdom who can find a way to help us continue the tradition that has kept this court alive to the joys of music,' he laments.

The vazir approaches him and says it is time for the darbar.

The king, queen, vazir enter the darbar. Citizens and courtiers rise in deference to the king. As the king walks through them, he is oblivious to all the beauty around him.

'Why,' the court wonders, 'is the king ignoring all that we have brought here for him to admire? Our art, our sculptures, our daughters, our wives – all ignored.'

Guruji comes in and pays obeisance.

'Come my old friend, there is little need for you to lie prostrate in front of us. You have but to ask, and what you want shall be given.'

Guruji rises and walks up to the king and whispers something in his ear. The king smiles.

'My lord vazir, will you conduct the darbar today. My friend has some news of great import, which can only be imparted in private. My apologies to all my fellow citizens and courtiers. We are sure your problems will be handled competently by my right hand in whom we place our trust.'

'Oh, friend of a thousand ragas, tell us this marvellous plan of yours that will make my son immortal in the world of music.'

'Your Highness, tomorrow morning the prince will be entranced by a sound so melodious that he will be compelled to follow it to its source. And then we shall see what he will be capable of.'

The next morning, just before sunrise, the prince sits on the rampart of the palace, doing his riyaaz. The sun rises, its first rays piercing through the early morning sky, as the prince launches into the Lalit raga. But he is barely into the alaap when he hears the pure tones of a woman's voice waft through the air. It is also the Lalit, but so pure in its rendering that the prince is dumbstruck.

He puts his tanpura down and follows the sound. Down the palace steps, into a private, secluded garden, and there in this garden, in a clear pool that could reflect the wings of a dragonfly, there is a vision.

She is about seventeen years old, immersed up to her waist in water. And, as she finishes the alaap, she comes out of the water, her skin translucent against the morning sun. She turns around and does the surya namaskar. When she raises her eyes, she sees the prince silhouetted against the sun.

'Listen! The gods themselves come down to bless me. The sun has answered my prayers. I thank you, oh Sun, for being the light to the world and the provider of all that is beautiful and good.'

The prince too turns and stretches his arms towards the sun.

'Oh, mighty Sun, this morning your warmth has spread to areas that knew no warmth earlier. I feel stirrings that I have never felt before. I expose myself to you so that your gentle rays can touch every part of me and make me aware of all that is wonderful and exquisite in nature.'

He turns to look at the girl, but she has disappeared. He looks behind a tree, a bush, but she's nowhere to be found. He rushes around the palace looking for her, but no one can help him. No one knows who he is talking about. It is now evening and he bursts into his guruji's chambers.

'Guruji, you who are so wise, you who know everything there is to know about this land and its people, you can tell me where I can find this vision that I saw this morning.'

Guruji looks at him with tenderness.

'My prince, only you can find the vision that is lodged in your heart. How can I, a mere purveyor of a few notes, help you?

Perhaps, if you told me more about this vision, I could make a few enquiries around the state.'

'Oh, guruji, words cannot describe what I have seen and felt.'

Guruji's wife enters, tanpura in hand, and sits behind the prince. She starts playing it. 'Then perhaps you can tell us with the help of music.'

The prince closes his eyes, anguish writ across his face, and bursts into a melody profound in its simplicity and in the rendering. Guruji is awestruck. He sits down, mouth hanging open. As the melody wafts through the palace moving from room to room, everybody is moved by the sadness that has filled the prince's heart.

The king and the queen in their private chambers hear in wonderment.

'My queen, who dares to sing with such beauty and sadness in my palace? Never have I heard such profound music. My heart bleeds for the singer and for me. Our union produced a prince, a master of all the ways of governing and science.'

'My king, you are perhaps a little too harsh on yourself, me, and our offspring. That voice you hear, which moves us to tears, is that of our youngest son.'

'If what you say is true let us visit the music chambers and seek out our newly-blessed son.'

'Before we do so, my lord, ask yourself what could produce such anguish, and be not disappointed if you learn the truth.'

'The truth? The truth is what one hears. Come, let us go and shower our son with all that he deserves.'

They leave their chambers and walk along the corridors of the palace. The corridors are lined with courtiers, all frozen in place, all listening to the prince. Slowly they make way for the king and queen. The court poet immortalizes that evening with a couplet, 'And though tears flowed down his face that evening, never had we seen such a radiant smile on the face of the king.'

They enter guruji's chambers just as the prince finishes his song. Though the king is in guruji's chamber, he throws decorum to the winds. He cannot contain his happiness and envelops guruji in an affectionate embrace, thanking him all the while for the joy he has brought to the palace and the kingdom.

'If anybody should be rewarded,' says guruji, 'let it be my wife, for it was her wisdom that brought this song about.'

'My son,' says the king, 'I do not wish to know what has given you the power to sing with such brilliance. It will suffice to say that today, music has finally, for the first time, shown its most beautiful face in this kingdom.'

The prince stares blindly all around him and then at the king. And he rushes out of the chamber. The whole court wonders what has happened.

Priamvade bows before the king.

'Your Highness, with your permission, may I speak? The prince is in the first throes of love. Slowly, he will encounter all the pain and pleasure of love. When he finally achieves manhood, the conquering of a woman, his talent will achieve full fruition. And that is what all of us here are waiting for.'

'Let it be soon,' says the king, 'so that the corridors of this palace can once again be full of melody and the joy that goes with it.'

Early next morning, the prince wanders along the palace corridors. He goes to the pond where he'd seen his vision. But she is not there. The king joins him and begs him to sing the morning raga. The prince looks at him as though he doesn't recognize him.

'You, my son, have so much to offer. You cannot hide your voice from the world.'

The prince looks stricken.

'You shall have my voice when I can find it, father.'

He rushes into the forest, leaving the king standing there looking forlorn.

Days go by. One evening while the prince leans listlessly against a tree, his dream girl walks past. She beckons to him and he follows her into a grotto. Inside, she disrobes.

'True love, oh prince, comes but once in a lifetime.'

She lowers all the lanterns in the grotto and invites him into a sunken tub. They cavort in the tub and, as he admires her physical beauty, he asks the obvious question. 'Who are you, oh lark of the morning? Why did you disappear for so long?'

'Hush,' she replies. 'Now is not the time for talk.'

She leads him to a bed and says she'll return in a moment. The lights dim further. After a few minutes, she slips into bed in the darkness, and instructs him on the art of kissing and touching. When he finally enters her, he starts singing a song so joyous that the birds outside the grotto join him.

'Never have I been so transported; never have I seen the worlds that you have shown me. You have changed my life. Ask anything of me and it shall be yours. But first promise me, my beloved, that you will stay by my side in bed and abroad for the rest of your life.'

And, in this joyous state again, he begins singing another song.

Meanwhile, outside the grotto, guruji is taking a walk. He hears the singing and wonders where it is coming from. He walks up to the grotto and pushes the branches that cover it, aside. He steps in and, in the morning light, sees the prince making love and singing. He admires the sight from behind a pillar. Delight is written all over his face. But, as the prince turns, so does the girl, and he sees it is his wife, Priamvade, her face ecstatic – more ecstatic than he has ever seen it before. He slowly staggers out.

Suddenly the singing loses all sense of harmony and the voice cracks. Guruji stops.

Inside the grotto, the prince has seen the woman he has been making love to.

'You … you … you are guruji's wife! Oh lord, what have I done? What have you done?'

'Sing for me,' she says. 'Think of the wonderful night you have spent, and sing for me.'

But he can't! All that comes out is a croak.

Guruji who, in the meantime, cannot contain himself any longer, bursts into the grotto.

'What has happened to your voice?' he demands.

'Fret not, oh lord of music,' his wife says. 'He never did have the capacity to make music as pure as our daughter's. It is for her sake that I have done this.'

The daughter, that vision who had lured the Prince to this bed, reappears.

'Surely you didn't expect me to sacrifice our daughter to the prince?' She turns towards him. 'My prince, you have learned more in one night than what it would take a lifetime to learn. Go and practice your new skills. They will stand you in much better stead than your voice.'

Guruji is in a rage. 'How could you do this?' he thunders.

And Priamvade, with a languorous smile, replies, 'With the greatest pleasure, my lord, with the greatest pleasure.'

Which is what I told my husband, my darling love, when he asked me how I could leave him and Calcutta.

Last night, dearest, was beautiful.

With much love, some regret and a sense of adventure,

I'm moving on.

Anila.

Mesho

Mesho decided he'd had enough.

Hari Prasad Coondoo, age seventy, aka Mesho, proprietor of the largest crockery and cutlery shop in the market, who was revered by all of us who were under eighteen as the only person in the previous generation worth listening to, had just finished his morning walk in Girish Park, a small patch of green nestled in the corner between Vivekanada Road and Chittaranjan Avenue.

In his stroll around the park, he'd met the regulars, said hello to them and then goodbye in the next breath.

He walked to the rose garden in the park and admired his favourites which were in the southwest corner of the rose garden. He stroked them very gently, leaned over to get a whiff of them and smiled wistfully. He turned reluctantly and walked out of the rose garden and though tempted to have a look once again, didn't.

He looked all around the park and thought of the number of Durga Pujas he had attended here and because of his erudition, had even presided over some of them. But he still preferred the puja that happened in his bari.

Of all the places in Calcutta he knew, this park was one of the two that he was going to miss. The other was Stratfordshire and Bros, the shop he had inherited in the New Market. 'I have a slightly odd family,' he used to tell me. 'Assuming that Stratfordshire is a geographical location, how can it have any brothers?'

A group of elderly ladies were discussing the best way to grind mustard. The eldest stopped mid-sentence as he walked past them. He had an aura about him that demanded silence. He walked out of the park and made his way to Mohun Bagan Lane where he knew his old friends would be waiting for him.

His tea arrived, accompanied with two hot, steaming kochooris. Today must be Wednesday, he thought to himself. On Wednesdays this is what they did, walked to Guha Babu's shop for his very non-Bengali khasta kochooris. On other days they went to other places, but all within walking distance of Guha Babu's establishment. Mesho took only one kochoori.

Messrs Ghosh, Mitter and Sanyal, his closest friends were engrossed in a fiery discussion of the previous day's football game which had turned out to be a triumph for East Bengal over their much beloved Mohun Bagan.

'Why only one?' Ghosh asked breaking off from the debate. Mesho just shrugged.

Mesho wasn't in the least interested in football but it did annoy him, as it had last night, that when East Bengal won, the price of ilish would double. Ilish was his favourite and he resented paying double for what he felt was no reason at all.

But that was last night. And since he'd relished his ilish the night before, it didn't really matter.

'It is time Chuni Goswami retired, don't you think?' he asked gently.

Conversation came to a halt. Messrs Ghosh, Mitter and Sanyal looked at him in surprise. He had never involved himself in the discussions on the finer, subtler points of football. And yet here he was, all three of them thought together, recommending that Chuni Goswami retire?

'Arre baba, don't look at me like I have murdered somebody.

Subimal has been playing since he was eight years old first for Mohun Bagan juniors and then for the seniors. Twenty-two years of relentless football is bound to take its toll. No?'

Sanyal who had just returned to Calcutta after spending nearly ten years in Scotland asked, 'Who is Subimal?'

'Chuni's bhalo naam is Subimal, didn't you know?' he asked Sanyal as he rose to settle the morning's bill. 'A request,' he continued, 'shall we meet tomorrow morning at my residence?'

Without waiting for an answer, he left.

Later that morning, he bounded into his shop with an energy that I had never seen before. He took a feather duster in one hand and a cloth duster in the other and proceeded to give the interiors of his shop a proper dusting and wipe down, all the while singing his favourite Nazrul songs and interspersing them with loud instructions for his minions. His word for his staff, used lovingly and without malice.

'Come my minions, join me for toast and tea,' he would often tell them. He would look across at our shop and at me. That would be my signal to go and take care of his establishment, while he took his 'minions' out.

Mesho had the shop opposite ours in the New Market.

My family sold dekchis of various kinds, steel, aluminium, brass and copper. All unbranded and by weight. Mesho's shop sold brands from all over the country and some brands from around the world.

And not just dekchis and bartans.

He imported some of the finest crystal from a city called Waterford in Ireland. I remember three distinct pieces that no one ever bought. They were exquisite and bloody expensive. There was a fascinating story attached to each one of them.

Every day, I used to rush to our shop after school. My father was very happy that at least one of his children (and he had many) was taking an interest in the business. It was only much later that he realized that I used to rush there to meet Mesho, hoping he had another tale to share.

There was a sense of real disappointment on days when Mesho didn't come to the shop. All of us in my age group used to find it 'hilariously funny' that he would often say 'Tomorrow, Mesho may not show.' We thought it was the height of sophisticated wit. He thought it was bad grammar. '"Hilariously funny?" No such thing,' he would growl, 'certainly not in any book of grammar penned by Messrs Wren and Martin.'

The crystal urn was his pride and joy. It was about a foot tall, exquisitely carved and when it caught the light at certain angles you believed all the stories Mesho told you about it.

According to him, over a period of time it had held the ashes of some of the most well-known literary and historical figures from around the world. The last person to occupy this urn, according to Mesho, was Engels, right until his ashes were scattered off Beachy Head near Eastbourne.

'Who was Engels?' I asked. I was twelve years old.

Up went his right eyebrow. It had a habit of doing that when it was surprised at your ignorance. And back went the crystal urn into its case.

'Arjun, you live in Calcutta and you do not know who Engels was? Go look him up and come back with all the information that you can. Then I will tell you the story of this historical urn and maybe even let you touch it.'

It took me a week to find out all I could about Engels and therefore Marx with him. When I returned and told Mesho that I have done my reading on Engels, he cross-examined me over the next few days and only when he was fully satisfied with my answers, did he hand the urn to me. I had earned the right to hold it.

While I sat there holding it, turning it, tilting it, and looking at it catch the light in Mesho's shop, he filled in all the blanks about Marx, Engels and the Industrial Revolution.

His embroidered stories about the urn were even more interesting. According to him, Wordsworth ended up in this urn about fifty years before Engels. Keats, and some of the lesser Romantics it is believed, had also been part-time residents before being scattered to the four winds. True or not, there was little about the Romantics I did not know, thanks to Mesho.

Of course it never occurred to me to ask why people whose 'good was oft interred with their bones' should end up incinerated and in this urn. 'If Engels could be incinerated why not the rest?' Why not indeed!

On a break from university, a few years later, I had gone walking in the Lake District and stumbled across Wordsworth's grave in Grasmere. I took a photograph of it and sent it to Mesho with a question scrawled behind it: From the urn to a grave?

When I returned to Calcutta from England, I walked into his shop and saw the photograph had been enlarged and framed, the urn was in a locked glass case, the front of it illuminated by a special spot light. The prismatic colours lit up the grave.

And below it was printed a 'Wordsworth-ian' legend: *Faith is a passionate intuition.*

I smiled.

He looked up from his khata.

'Phirechho?' he said. 'Besh!' ('You're back? Good!')

One of my favourite pieces in his shop was the 'crystal serving plate with an ornately carved crystal dome cover' that he had. One evening, around the time the shops were closing in the New Market, he called my father and me over for what he called the Grand Experience.

When we walked in, we discovered the central area of the shop had been cleared of all the cartons of stuff that used to be displayed. Parked there instead was a deep, dark mahogany table. On it was the 'ornately carved crystal dome cover' right next to a large, fat candle whose flame danced as it reflected off the crystal ware.

The table was set for three. We sat around the table. Something red was visible through the 'ornately carved crystal dome'.

'I have to tell you that even the Queen of England has a favourite place for eating Indian dishes. It is a very upmarket restaurant in Regents Street. She always orders Britain's favourite dish – chicken tikka masala,' he said un-doming as it were, the crystal plate.

On it was a steaming chicken tikka masala.

We each took two pieces on our Wedgwood plates.

'The last time she ate this it was served to her in this Waterford set which is now on sale here. You dear Arjun Babu,' he said ruffling my hair, 'are having dinner that is fit for the Queen. Rumour has it that ever since this set came into my possession, she has never enjoyed a tikka masala,' he said licking the last remnants of the masala off his fingers with great pleasure. 'Silly woman. What's one got to do with the other!'

Truth or fiction? It didn't matter.

One thing was clear, in fact crystal clear. He was as passionate a fan of crystal as he was of the English and as he was of the Queen. Just last year, I noticed him supervising the re-painting of a slogan on one of the glass showcases at the entrance of his shop: BY APPOINTMENT TO HER MAJESTY in an elaborate Gingerbread Victorian font that had more curlicues in it than Bob Marley's dreads.

The hurricane vase was the third piece he possessed that received the same kind of importance as the other two. It was an exquisite vase shaped like a hurricane lamp. I am assuming that is why it was called hurricane.

He meant to tell us about it. But tragedy struck quite unexpectedly on one of his 'Mesho, may not show' days.

A gentleman from Sri Lanka walked into his shop, made an obscene cash offer for it and the poor unsuspecting salesman who just happened to be one of Mesho's innumerable nephews, and who had not been briefed yet, let it go.

Neither the lamp nor the Sri Lankan gentleman was seen again. And the nephew-salesman disappeared along with them. According to my father, Mesho took him to the Burma border, handed him over to yet another family in exile, and told him never to show his face on Indian territory again.

He never did tell us about the hurricane vase.

Every three or four years, Mesho would disappear with the arrival of the monsoons on a yatra and be back in Calcutta in time for Durga Puja.

This was odd because while people of his age usually went to tirthsthans, he went on subject yatras.

He did go on one tirthyatra once and though a deeply religious man, swore on all the religious sites he visited that that would be the last one he'd ever go on. 'By and large,' he confided, 'a tirthyatra is an extremely unhygienic exercise.'

He'd heard about tanchoi sarees so one year he disappeared on a choi yatra. He traced the route the silk took from the Choi brothers in China to the ancestral homes of the three Gujarati gentlemen who brought the silk to India.

Three is tran in Gujarati; from tran to tan is an easy mispronunciation especially for the Bengali; hence tanchoi. To this day I do not know which had the better weave – the tanchoi saree or his story!

I bumped into him in a shop one pre-monsoon trying on a pair of swimming trunks. Now Mesho trying on swimming trunks is not something anyone wants to see more than once in a lifetime. Trust me.

There was a square pillar in the centre of the shop, each side had a mirror attached to it and in front of one of the mirrors, of course it had to be the one facing the entrance. Mesho had raised his panjabi, put on a pair of bright red trunks over his dhoti and was admiring his not insignificant posterior.

'I am off to measure the waves on the west coast,' he

announced. 'Dheyuyatra (a journey on the waves),' he said. He asked the shopkeeper to wrap three of the trunks that fit him and disappeared for the next four months.

He took a train and reached Porbandar after many train changes along the way.

'Gandhiji got his idea of the salt march here, I thought I should start my monsoon march from here.'

Wherever he could, he walked. The rest of the time he'd catch a bus or hitch a ride to the next beach. He met as he put it, non-Bengalis of all shapes, sizes and colours, both exquisitely beautiful and ugly, and swam, notwithstanding the monsoons, at every beach he visited.

Isn't it amazing how only Bengalis meet 'non-Bengalis' on their travels? You are not a Maharashtrian, or Gujarati, or Goan or Kannadiga! Or even an Indian. You are, if you are not a Bengali, a non-Bengali.

'What about the waves?' I remember asking him.

And being the true Bengali that he was, he replied, 'The waves and the cuisine along the west coast are not worth writing home about, so I didn't. Nothing like the waves of the Bay of Bengal or Bengali food. Wonderful people though.'

When he and his 'minions' returned from their cup of tea, he sat me down and very quietly without any fanfare or flourish, handed me the urn and the crystal serving plate with dome.

'These are for you,' he said. 'Two of my favourite pieces. They're yours to do with what you will.'

I tried refusing them. I knew how much he treasured them but no luck. 'You were meant to have them and you shall.' I looked across to my father in our shop. 'I have spoken to your father about it already so there is no need to take his permission.' One part of me said I shouldn't have them. They belonged to Mesho. They were so much a part of his life. The other part coveted them, not for their shelf value but for all the lovely stories associated with them.

Very reluctantly, I took these wonderful pieces of crystal and walked to my father.

'Why?'

'Sometimes, my son, it is prudent not to ask for an explanation or to expect one,' he said. 'Now attend to Mrs Mukherjee. She needs some stainless steel water glasses,' he said as he handed over his favourite customer to me.

I do not know what Mesho was up to. But one thing was for certain, I was soon going to find out.

It was New Year's Eve and I had a party to go to. Mesho and his odd behaviour could wait until the New Year.

Now most bad news comes in at four in the morning and over the years, people have come to fear the four am call.

But that dreaded call that usually came in at four am, didn't.

It came in at about three.

The phone rang.

And it rang incessantly.

I was pretty sozzled from the party I'd attended earlier and had just floated away into a not unpleasant dream in which I was the centre of attention in a fight with a villainous black dog.

Both the villainous black dog in my dream and I looked at the clock.

Five minutes to three.

My dreams are like Hindi movies with bad English sub-titles. They are usually pirated VHS tapes manufactured in Dubai which are sub-titled there too. And sent back to India on the Thursday before the Friday release of the movie.

In my dreams I can't hear what is being said even when *I'm* saying it. I can read the subtitles though and I had just finished telling the four-legged canine, 'Kutte main tera khoon pee jaaoonga! (Dog! I will drink your blood!)

The villainous black dog looked at me, drooling and frothing at the mouth, still glancing at the clock in my dream. 'Mr Danga and Mr Phasaad will spread to four sides of the country,' it barked silently at me via the subtitles. ('Danga aur phasaad desh ke charon taraph phail jayenge!' is what I lip-read.) Do you see what I mean about the rather suspect quality of the sub-titling?

The dog knocked the phone off the cradle with its snout but the phone kept ringing.

I woke up.

It was *my* phone ringing loudly into the night.

It had to be Koely. Only she of all my friends would have the courage to break the four am emergency time barrier.

And she was Mesho's daughter.

'Koely, go back to bed,' I mumbled into the phone as I tried to get the taste of sleep and cheap whisky out of my mouth.

'I need you here. Now.'

It *was* Koely. She sounded distressed.

This had been going on for a long time now. At least once a year, Koely would encounter a crisis and for some odd reason (very odd) she felt that I was the best person to help her overcome whatever it was.

I have been known in Calcutta … in fact I have a reputation there as being absolutely the last person to call in a crisis.

Everybody except Koely knew that.

'It's my father. He's going to die.'

'We all are Koely.'

'But he says he is going to die at the end of the next three days!' she cried.

Perhaps that explained the dream I was having. If anything happened to Mesho, 'Mr Danga' and 'Mr Phasaad' would certainly take over the New Market and shut it down. We were at that age when at the slightest pretext or imagined slight, eight or ten of us would go around the market making sure shutters were downed for the day.

Koely and I had been friends since our kindergarten years in a girls' convent on Middleton Row. Yes, yes, they used to allow boys of that age in their school. Even Jyoti Basu was there a generation or so before I was. And look what happened to him, I can hear you exclaim. It has got to be said that the nuns there were famous for driving you to despair or communism.

She lived in the Burrabazaar side of town, so from the New Market area where I lived, it took a couple of hours to walk. There were no cabs available, taxi drivers refused to stir at that hour. In fact they were famous for refusing to go anywhere even during the day. Buses hadn't begun their routes yet and the only way to get there was by rickshaw or car. Since I didn't drive, I couldn't take the family car and since I refused to take a rickshaw on principle, I had to walk.

She lived in one of those three-storeyed (ground plus two) North Calcutta homes which were built around a central courtyard where all the family functions and Durga Pujas used to be celebrated.

At any given time there were at least sixty-five people – Koely's parents, aunts, uncles, nieces, nephews, bahus and even the occasional gharjamai for good measure – living in the house.

Over a period of time, I had met all of them and they were easily the most disjointed joint family I had ever come across.

The huge house just swallowed them whole.

Normally one never saw any one there except the person you wanted to see, in my case it was usually Koely. Sometimes when she was late coming down from the second floor, I was escorted to her father's room by one of her relatives. A rare honour I was told some years later. He hated meeting people who wasted his time on this earth. But I was his young friend from the market so I was permitted in to his 'hallowed presence.'

I reached there around five in the morning, just as the first tram of the day trundled past their home. Five am is not too early by Calcutta's standards but definitely too early for the mayhem that met me when I walked in.

The first thing that you notice when you walked in was the amazing architecture of the house. I'd seen it many times but it surprised me every time. A central courtyard surrounded by a building made of bright red plaster and stone. Yellow railings and archways. This morning the holy Jagannath trinity on the parapet of the second floor, looking directly down at the courtyard, was adorned with flowers ready for a puja of sorts.

January the first seemed the wrong date for a puja for Balaram, Subhadra and Jagannath. But there they were, resplendent with garlands and all the accoutrements that went with a puja.

The central courtyard was swarming with at least a hundred or so family members and friends.

Volume levels were high. This was not some place someone was dying in! This sounded and felt like a beeye bari.

Instructions were being issued left, right and centre. Instructions that no one was following. So the decibels rose by the minute.

And here was something I had never seen before.

Directly underneath the Jagannath trinity, laid out in the courtyard, was a four-poster bed bedecked with flowers of every kind, each getting the individual attention of Bose Babu, our friendly neighbourhood florist from New Market.

I tracked Koely down, she was in her room on the second floor and asked her what the hell was going on.

'Let's go meet Baba,' she said and took me into his room.

I had prepared myself to see a frail old man connected to various bottles through various tubes.

Mesho was looking as far away from death as you can imagine.

He was dressed in just a dhoti, bare bodied, pacing up and down in his room like an angry bull with an energy I had not seen in a long time.

That he was angry would be putting it mildly.

The only time I'd seen him angrier was when the hurricane vase had been sold by mistake. I wondered who was going to end up in Burma this time.

'Namaskar Mesho, you don't look like you're going to die in a hurry.'

'Arjun,' he said even more angry, 'you are grown up now, you really must do something about that cheap whisky you drink. Your breath can kill an elephant at fifty paces.'

'And a very happy new year to you too,' I said sarcastically, 'Koely, I'm obviously not needed. Don't call me at least until the next century.'

I turned to leave but Mesho had beaten me to the door. He closed it, turned around and looked imploringly at me. His anger had disappeared.

'Stay. Please.'

He was Mesho. And a favourite. I shouldn't have taken umbrage. 'Mesho, what were you so angry about?'

I looked at him. This was not the Mesho I knew. There was a sense of bewilderment and barely concealed excitement as if he was searching for something in unfamiliar territory.

'Oooof! Families! They won't let a man die in peace. Now why don't you freshen up while we arrange for some breakfast? Koely, give him one of my freshly laundered dhoti-panjabis to wear. Do it Arjun. It's important you stay.'

By the time I was showered and ready, a 'table' had been laid out for three, banana leaves with a little paati lebu, kaacha lanka and noon in place, on the floor of a room called the Gorur Ghar.

Though Mesho sold the finest crockery and cutlery in the world, he ate off kala pata. 'Bangla ranna just does not taste Bangla if it is not consumed off a kala pata!' he would exclaim while wiping off the last morsel of food from the banana leaf with his index finger. 'Crystal plates are splendid to sell, and marvellous to admire. But for eating? Kala pata!'

We settled down to eat in the Gorur Ghar. In all the years I had known Mesho and Koely, this was the first time I had been in this room. An odd name for a room one would have thought but not so if you walked in. The walls were lined with glassed-in shelves with cow curiosities from all over the world – Krishna cows, Jersey cows, Texan cows, short cows from Assam – you name a region and there was a cow from there; cows made from stone, clay, bronze, and from every material known to man. There was even a jewel-encrusted one. This was a weird place to be eating breakfast in on New Year's Day.

The maharaj brought in the first course, deep fried rui maachh with some kashundi if you needed it. Let us not forget, that it was now nearly six in the morning. For the life of me I couldn't imagine how I was going to let any deep-fried items pass my lips so early in the morning after the kind of night I'd had. A rui maachh wasn't my cup of tea. In fact even a cup of tea wasn't. I hadn't had a damned cup of coffee yet.

'Maharaj, aamader jonne chai, Arjun babu coffee khaabe.'

He bit into his maachh with relish and started talking about his latest holiday. He'd gone to Kashi in June and had got back about a week ago.

What on earth had he been doing there for the last six months?

I waited for the coffee.

Mesho concentrated on what remained of his breakfast. I bit tentatively into my maachh bhaja but still couldn't stomach it. I was a bit worried about Koely. She had a permanent frown furrowed on to her forehead, which was very unlike her.

'My shehnai yatra was initially a bit of a letdown.'

'Mesho, what on earth is a shehnai yatra … were you looking for a shehnai or types of shehnais? I mean they are available here in Beadon Street. Why do you have to go to Varanasi?'

'Arre Arjun Babu, Khan Saheb, the world's greatest exponent of the shehnai! Ooof! Koely how could you have befriended such a moron?'

'The question, Baba, is how could you?' she replied.

'Anyway, I reached Kashi, took a dip in the Ganga, irreligious or not, one has to take a dip in the Ganga, and made my way straight to his house in Sarai Harha and introduced myself.'

'What can I do for you?' Khan Saheb asked.

'Nothing,' I replied. 'Nothing today. I have just arrived from Calcutta and I wanted to visit you.'

'I am very happy that you have come to visit me, my friend from Calcutta,' he said smiling, 'but it would be of great assistance if you told me who you were. Do I know you?'

'Haripada Coondoo is my name,' I told him. 'I am going to be here for the next six months or so. I thought I would visit you and pay my respects. I wish to come every day and listen to you do your riyaaz.'

'That is sad. You see we are going on a foreign tour which is about a month long,' Khan Saheb said. 'We shall be leaving in about an hour.'

'I was disappointed and some of the disappointment must have been visible on my face,' Mesho said.

'But all is not lost, Coondoo Babu,' said Khan Saheb. 'I will see you at seven in the morning, on the tenth of August in front of the Viswanath temple. Please wait for me there.'

Mesho concentrated on what remained of his breakfast. He would get to the point of his story in time. The maharaj brought in their tea and my coffee. Their tea was served in bhands – untreated, unbaked clay cups – my coffee came in a black mug with the word 'Belladona' printed on it in white.

'One of my suppliers sent this to me from England. I have six such with Arsenic, Cyanide, Belladona et cetera printed on them. They are for when you visit. I do not understand the humour of names of poisons on mugs but I am certain there are people who do.'

I took another sip of my coffee and thought about why Mesho had told us this story. What was it all about? What was the purpose? Was the story over or was there more to it?

'Mesho, what does your visit to Kashi have to do with dragging me here in the middle of the night?

He took a deep satisfying sip of his tea, smacked his lips, and as he helped himself to a mouthful of steaming hot radhavallabhi and alu dum that the maharaj had brought, and said, 'He was there on August the tenth at seven in the morning. Waiting for me.'

He had a dreamy look on his face. He wasn't here anymore. He was back in Varanasi.

'For the next four and a half months, until last week, I was with him at any given time of the day or night. Khan Saheb would call me over at the oddest of hours and say 'ye suno.' When you have heard Khan Saheb playing the Raga Paraj at two in the morning, the Raga Multani at two in the afternoon and every raga in between at the times the ragas should be played and heard – the Multani in the late afternoon, the Poorvi at dusk, the Shahana at midnight,' he said ending in a tihai of 'et cetera et cetera et cetera, what else is there to live for?'

I looked at him with envy, a good envy I might add, because if anybody deserved this pleasure it was Mesho.

'When you have experienced what I have and when you have eaten and drunk your share of the world's resources, and when you have breathed your share of the earth's air, it is not fair to continue living. I have therefore decided that it is time to move on.'

Koely who had been silent all this while finally spoke. 'Baba has been driving me mad, Arjun. From the moment he's come back all he is talking about is taking samadhi.' She turned to Mesho, 'Baba, this is a bad joke that will come back to haunt you …' Koely started to say.

'Indeed it is. And so is death. A bad joke on life,' Mesho cut in. 'Now listen Koely, I want this to be a fun funeral. Either get into it with gusto or go away for a few days.'

At a 'Last Lunch' where his large extended family was present, in front of a spread that would have been the envy of any king, after a loud, satisfied belch, Mesho announced his plans and his death.

'On this earth, I have eaten my quota of solids, consumed my quota of liquids, and breathed enough of its foul air. As of this moment I shall not be a burden on the earth's limited resources anymore. I relinquish all food, all drink and on the third day from today, I shall breathe the last bit of air that I am entitled to.'

And so began three days of crying, laughing, beating of breasts, wailing and chaos. The grand farce.

His 'death' was announced in the papers and he took his place on the four-poster bed under the holy trinity. Friends, relatives, well-wishers and some gloaters arrived to mourn his 'death.' He chatted to all of them. A lot of them understood what he was doing. Others thought he was mad. Koely and I sat up with him that night. The rest had gone to bed. 'And why not,' he told us. 'Most of my life people have either understood what I've wanted to do or thought I was crazy. This is fun.'

The next morning three pandits, their heads shaven, dressed in orange, trooped in with their musical instruments, and parked themselves at the foot of his bed and started singing bhajans.

I have a problem with what I call high Bengali, the literary language with the 'hoiyachhays' and the 'koriyachhays' that people use in their writings and sometimes speech. The bhajans were like that and it took me a while to understand what was being rendered.

I would not like to malign Mesho in any way since he was one of my all-time favourite people, so it will suffice to say that some of the bhajans were the funniest (and filthiest, I might add) bhajans I had ever heard, composed and penned by Mesho just for the occasion.

Dehotyag kor-i-ben Haripada Coondoo
'Kesh-tyag' korilo aamader mundu

The closest translation I can come up with, with my limited Bengali would be:

When Haripada Coondoo sacrificed himself dead
We sacrificed the hairs on our head.

The bawdy bhajans were a bit too bawdy to put down on paper and in memory of the Mesho I knew, I am going to leave them out of this narrative.

He had obviously been working on the songs for some time and had even rehearsed them with his 'pandit' friends who sang them with the appropriate pious expressions on their faces. On closer inspection I noticed they were all from his morning walk gang – Messrs Ghosh, Mitter and Sanyal. Now all completely bald.

'No one knew I was going to come into this world but by God they will know that I'm leaving it,' Mesho proclaimed loudly to anyone that cared to listen.

And they did.

It was the silly season, not much was happening in the world and a newly published Bengali newspaper got hold of the news. They rushed to the Coondoo house and after much cajoling and persuasion were led into Mesho's presence. The newspaper shut down after a year or so but this one story did keep it afloat for a while. It is not surprising to note that bad journalism then was just as bad as bad journalism now. Though the earnestness with which the interview was conducted cannot be faulted for any lack of sincerity. Whoever wrote the headline to the story deserves an award:

CALCUTTA'S CROCKERY KING TO CREMATE SELF in ninety-six point Garamond Bold across the width of page three. In tandem with the sub-headline it was even more intriguing: CONFESSES ALL IN EXCLUSIVE INTERVIEW.

Over the next two days, whenever Mesho had a spare moment, he would describe little vignettes from his childhood.

'According to the oral history of the Coondoo family, of which my Naupishima was the keeper,' he started, 'my fifty-year-old mother Sitadevi Coondoo, was admitted to a hospital in Central Avenue in the afternoon, on 4 August 1898, with an abnormally large tumour and an excruciating pain in her lower abdomen.'

No one could quite diagnose what was wrong with her and during a rather thorough examination conducted by the hospital's head surgeon, she went into paroxysms of pain and uncontrolled spasms.

A few minutes later with a little help from the surgeon and nurses and with a shriek of pain that stopped the traffic on Central Avenue, she expelled the tumour.

My father who was in the waiting room of the hospital when he heard the shriek did what any self-respecting sixty-five-year-old man would do in a similar situation. He fainted.

My mother who was plump to begin with should have been menopausal. Everyone thought she was. She thought she was. The fact that the tumour was a healthy eight pound one, kicking and screaming for all it was worth – came as an unpleasant little surprise. Well, maybe not so little.

And so I was born.

My eldest sister who was a freshly-minted house surgeon in the hospital at the time and who was by mother's bedside, didn't know where to look. To be lumbered with a baby brother at the age of twenty-two must have been more than a bit embarrassing.

When my father awoke, he found himself in a hospital bed in the maternity ward, my mother Sitadevi sitting beside him in the visitor's chair with a smile on her face and I at her breast suckling away as if there was no tomorrow. Though he did manage not to faint at the sight of his son, it was a long time before he spoke again.

The truth was that even though the sight of his fifty-year-old wife feeding a newborn sent him into a 'near-fatal second fainting fit', as he liked to put it, like all men, he too was ecstatic that finally, after six daughters his wife had borne him a son. This was the son who was going to put the Coondoo name where it belonged – 'in the minds' eye of people who mattered.'

Baba, Mesho continued his story, was one of those regular New Market folks I came to discover as I grew older under his aegis. Bardhan Babu, as he was called by all the others in the market, sat in his shop Stratfordshire and Bros from nine every morning to eight every night amidst some of the most exquisitely designed and manufactured crockery and cutlery from around the world. No one except he was allowed to handle the delicate pieces that were artistically displayed around the shop.

When I was about four, Baba walked into Ma's room where I was surrounded by my sisters and my mother. I was dressed in a faded pink dress which belonged to my eldest sister, the doctor, one of the first women doctors in Calcutta in fact, and dancing to songs they were singing to me.

He took one look at what was going on, turned around, went to his shop and handed the reins of Stratfordshire and Bros to his clumsy brothers. He presented each brother with a pair of kid-leather gloves in the hope that they would wear them while handling the delicate crockery on display. It was meant to be a joke but his brothers who had all at some time or the other faced his rather irrational wrath, took the gloves seriously. It must be remembered that the New Market was at the best of times, hot, humid and sweaty. For many years after, until I took over the business, the shop smelled smelt faintly of wet leather.

He took over my life. Mind you, there was a bit of a struggle. My mother felt that I needed her gentle touch in my upbringing. My father felt I needed a swift kick in the pants.

Battle lines were drawn.

From the women of the house who took care of me for the first four years of my life, six lovely elder sisters and a slightly crazy mother who indulged my every whim, I was transferred to the care of Baba and his major domo.

Off Harrison Road where we lived was not as crowded then as it became later. It was a fairly broad, tree-lined street with large houses on either side. One could never make out how large the houses really were from the outside. In the Coondoo home, the antar mahal which was the domain of the women of the house, was connected by a maze of covered pathways that led to the Ganga nearly a mile away. The women of the house who were 'untouched by sunlight' and, except for my sisters, who were also untouched by the twentieth century, were not supposed to be 'influenced by the outside world', would take these covered lanes to the river for their daily Ganga snan. The place was off limits for me.

Harrison Road wasn't.

Very early, every morning, a family of gowalas delivered fresh milk to the houses that required it. Each gowala was responsible for one cow. He would bring it to the entrance of his customer's house where a large bucket or milk can would be waiting for him. He'd milk the cow for the required quantity, give it a pat on its back and the cow would meander over to the next customer's house and wait patiently for the gowala to catch up.

Cows tend to do that.

The gowala would collect his money, make a little conversation and move to the next house to start the whole process again. This had been going on for years and the householders, gowalas and cows had come to accept this as an almost religious ritual.

But all things must change.

And now by the time the gowala collected the money and turned around to move to the next house, the cow wasn't chewing its cud where it normally did but was seen charging down the road.

Soon, over a period of a week, his fellow gowalas also began complaining of the same odd behaviour of their cows as well.

In the second week, none of the cows would even enter that section of Harrison Road. They stood at the head of the road and dug their heels into the ground, mooing and bellowing loudly much to the consternation of the residents. The gowalas were pulling at their leads trying to drag them to their various stations along the way. But with little success. The mooing and bellowing grew louder and the crowd grew larger.

Suddenly a small figure, arms and legs flailing all over the place, jumped off a lamppost nearby, right on top of the lead cow yelling at the top of its voice, 'Aami cowboy, aami cowboy.'

I was now about six years old and had decided I wanted to be a cowboy.

The lead cow took off with a loud bellow with me clinging on for dear life, followed closely by the rest, followed even more closely by the gowalas and the residents with their buckets and milk cans clanging loudly against each other. It was perhaps the oddest chase anyone had ever seen.

Somewhere in my young, confused head I thought cowboys rode cows and had for the last fortnight, tried to get onto any one of them. I'd shin up a lamp post, cling to the top, wait patiently for the cow to arrive and then jump on it. The cow would be so startled it would run away dislodging me almost immediately. Until that day when I managed to cling on and lead the charge as it were.

Of course this meant the birch rod awaited me upon my return home!

Many younger members of the Coondoo family had been at

the business end of a much used birch rod that hung behind the door to Bardhan Babu's room. On this day Bardhan Babu waited for me to come into the room and receive my punishment. I walked in, rubbing my bum, ruefully saying, 'Baba aita kalke kari? Gorur peeth ta quite sakta actually.' (Baba can we do this tomorrow? A cow's back is quite hard actually.)

Whether it was the expression on my face or the fact that this was the first time my father had heard me use the word 'actually' with such confidence, he laughed and his laughter could be heard up and down Harrison Road. He put the birch rod behind the door and there it has stayed since, unused to this day.

I never tried to ride a cow again but the damage had been done and that is why one rarely sees a cow on Harrison Road.

Over the years this episode with a cow took on epic proportions and was perhaps responsible for the development of the Gorur Ghar .

And this is how it began.

Keshto Kaka, one of my innumerable kakas, had gone to Mathura and came back with a statuette of a cow. I was thinking of my experience with the Harrison cows, and I smiled when I saw it. Keshto Kaka who had brought nothing else for me from Mathura gave it to me.

'For you, especially, all the way from Mathura.'

'Besh!' I said and kept it.

For the next few days, as is a child's wont, I kept the cow close to me, spoke to it, fed it, had imaginary adventures with it and even kept it next to my bed at night it in a little Bata shoe box with a little bit of straw acquired from one of the packing cases from the shop.

Keshto Kaka was thrilled that Borda's little 'afterthought' as I was called, loved the cow and told his wife who told all the other relatives who lived in the forty-plus rooms.

Thereafter, whomsoever went out anywhere, whether it was just around the corner to Tiretti bazaar or to Texas, USA, brought back some kind of cow for me.

I was quite astounded by their lack of imagination. After receiving the three-hundredth cow I asked my father with a slightly puzzled look, 'Baba, are all my kakas and kakimas aware that there are more things in life than statues of cows?'

Even though I made it quite clear in no uncertain terms (Cows look so stupid, na kakima?) the cows kept coming. Soon they went straight to the cow-room which over a period of time grew shelves, display cases, and nooks and crannies to house all the cows that came in and the room soon became a proper noun – Gorur Ghar.

I was the 'proud' and rather disgruntled owner, at the last count which happened when I was around fourteen years old, of about two-thousand-eight-hundred and fifty-three utterly useless cows. Over the years the occasional new cow will somehow still find its way into the collection but not to the Gorur Ghar. It is relegated to the basement in its wrapping paper without my getting even a glimpse of it.

Sitadevi Coondoo, my mother, however had been promoted to Queen Bee status for providing a son and heir to the Harrison Road household after producing six rather successful daughters – the first three were doctors of medicine, of physics and of zoology. The rest were in various stages of higher education.

Ever since the rather 'tumourous' birth of their brother, after the initial embarrassment especially for Padma the eldest, who happened to be on call at the hospital when Sitadevi was admitted with a tumour and left with me, I had been spoiled and pampered by all my siblings. And Sitadevi, as a reward, had been sent on a worldwide cruise of religious shrines.

It had been almost a year since she had left and was currently in Paris visiting the Chapel of Our Lady of the Miraculous Medal at 140 Rue du Bac, one of the many places where the Virgin Mother visited St Catherine who now lies there in a glass coffin.

How religious Sitadevi really was, was another matter. The only reason she was visiting 140 Rue du Bac was the medal. She liked the design and thought it would look elegant if printed on a tea pot. There was little doubt that she was my father's wife.

Behind that large, placid exterior of a North Calcutta ginni, was not just a mind, but a mind that functioned far more effectively than people gave it credit for.

'I was certain,' she confided to a friend as she readied her daily quota of paans, 'that my work as a mother was done. Then out of nowhere came this horrible little monster. Please don't look shocked. He was my son, our son and I loved him unabashedly. But I did *not* have to *like* him! As soon as my husband took charge of Hari's upbringing, I decided it was time for a yatra. ('Perhaps it was from my dear mother that I developed this thirst for travelling!') So off I went.'

'I received the information of his cow episode in Paris. He was obviously being thoroughly indulged and spoiled. So I sprinkled some gangajal on St Catherine's glass coffin,' she said as she sprinkled some essence on each of the paans, 'and came home. I am glad I did because the boy was getting absolutely out of hand.'

'How did you get the gangajal in Paris?' her friend asked puzzled.

'I always carry ten gallons of it when I travel, don't you know,' she said nonchalantly. 'Once you sprinkle gangajal on the shrines, they become more acceptable, do you see what I mean?' she said with a mischievous look in her eye.

'What are you going to do?' her friend asked.

Sitadevi took two paans, parked them firmly into her left cheek and with more than just a determined gleam in her eye said, 'Take back charge. I am going to take back charge.'

'And how did she take back charge?' Mesho asked us. 'By the good old system that has worked very well in this and every other family that I know – bribery and corruption. She gave me a bicycle and told me that the minute I learned how to ride it she would buy up every single rosogolla from Nobin Chandra Das' tiny little shop in Baghbazar. These days we take the rosogolla so much for granted but then the rosogolla had just been invented by Nobin Babu and was easily the most sought after mishti of the time.'

'Two days later there was a mini riot in our home. You see, I had learned how to ride the cycle and Ma, as promised, had bought up Nobin Babu's stock. Baba stood on the verandah just above my head under the Jagannath trinity laughing quietly to himself, and Ma stood where I am now, trying to placate an irritated crowd of irate neighbours who had been deprived of their daily dose of the magical mishti. The neighbours left only after Ma assured them that she would pay for Nobin Babu's entire stock the next day and they could collect their share for free from him. Nobin Babu who was there, readily agreed to get the next day's stock ready as early as was possible. The neighbours began applauding.'

'Now here is a little aside to this tale which has got nothing to do with anything. The Saha family which was visiting that day were on their way out when they heard my Ma's announcement. The elder Mr Saha stopped at the main doorway, turned around and glared at the assembly.'

'Nobin Babu,' his voice boomed across the courtyard, 'give everybody here notun gurer shondesh too, on my account.'

'And he sailed out of the house secure in the knowledge that he had bested the Coondoo family once again in some useless rivalry that began no one knows when.'

'My father by now had tears rolling down his cheeks, his rather ample torso jiggled with every breath of laughter that came out of him. My mother was, to say the least, enraged. Her anger was not directed at Saha Babu, but at her husband's now uncontrollable fit of laughing.'

'They didn't speak for days after.'

'They were so silent they forgot me completely. I was restless. Which suited me very well since I took this opportunity to explore the surroundings on my cycle. Normally a child of six or was I four, I forget now, was not permitted to leave the Coondoo home unaccompanied by an adult. On day one, I ventured out and about fifteen minutes of furious pedalling towards the river, I found myself at Nimtallah Ghat.'

'Perhaps these early visits to the cremation grounds at Nimtallah is what made me study death with such interest. I have always been intrigued by it. Not by the actual fact of death but by the circus that surrounds it, the wailing and the beating of breasts, I think I knew at that age that there was something not quite right about the rituals that accompanied death.'

'If one has to die, then one must die like this. Surrounded by one's loved ones, celebrating death, rushing towards it with all one's faculties intact.'

Maharaj came into the courtyard wheeling in a trolley full of food. Snacks for the mourners.

Friends, relatives and guests piled on the food like they hadn't eaten for weeks. Mesho watched the proceedings with a benign smile on his face. He was enjoying every moment. He would occasionally take a morsel of food and put it into a child's mouth.

We were on the first floor, Koely and I, looking down at the courtyard.

'Is there a way to stop this madness?' Koely asked.

'I don't think so. One of the few things I know about Mesho is that when he makes his mind up about something, there is little that can change it.'

'We can always call the police you know and call it an "attempted suicide" which is the legal way out of it.'

'And what do you think Mesho will do when he finds out it's you who complained?'

'I don't want to think about it,' Koely said and we let the matter drop.

Late that night, after the guests had left Mesho requested the family to go to bed. 'I need you fresh for tomorrow,' he told them. 'There is much to be done. I have no intentions of dying until the day after.' Koely, Mesho and I were the only ones awake in that now empty central courtyard.

'Mesho, is there a way I can make you change your mind? There is so much more I have to learn from you.'

'Arjun, there is nothing more I have to give, if ever there was anything at all. I have only one last request, though. Go to the station in the morning and pick up Khan Saheb and his entourage. Koely, let them stay in my set of rooms. I have no use for them.'

And so, from the moment they arrived, Khan Saheb and his entourage played for Mesho. They set up their 'stage' near Mesho's bed and through the day and into the next morning played the appropriate raga for the time of day.

'As they would say in your language Arjun, this is a regular raga around the clock, wouldn't you agree?'

And so on day three in the early morning as Khan Saheb moved from the Sohini into the Lalit, Mesho moved on from this world into the next.

His urn with his ashes sits in my shop window keeping an eye as it were over Stratfordshire and Bros.

And over us.

Acknowledgements

There are more than a million people I have to say thank you to for making this volume of Calcutta short stories possible, especially those who live in and around the New Market, have shops there and have made that whole area as vibrant as it is.

If you recognize yourselves, forgive me. The stories I have written around your characters are just that – stories. Works of fiction inspired by a few words you've said, or some stray thoughts you've had which have been filed away in the recesses of my memory and have been dredged up to fill these pages.

I am sure all of you would have looked much better on film and who knows, you still might.

To my family – Gulan, Pushan and Rehana whom I have embarrassed incessantly over the years and who fervently hope that this book will not add to their embarrassment. Thank you for being there through the good times and the bad, propping me up when I needed it, and pulling me down to earth when I floated out of my under-sized boots.

To Aparna (Babli) – for standing by like a rock, always there when I needed support. And to Ma (Kamal Sanyal) for never criticizing my erratic behaviour even when I felt that she wanted to.

Divya Dubey, who befriended me on Facebook. Believe it or not, we have interacted only on Facebook and have never met each other, face to face. I think of her as an old friend without whose interruptions (at various times over the last few months) I would never have thought of completing these stories. Thank you so much Divya, you old nag!

When Saugata Mukherjee of Pan Macmillan India showed an interest in the book, I thought he was kidding. Thanks Saugata, for keeping the faith and giving me the confidence to write the last story.

My mother, god rest her soul, would have loved reading some of these stories, had she been around. And there were many neighbourhood secrets she let me into which have found their way into these stories. My siblings Padma, Kamla, Pramila, Uttam and Sajni have at various times threatened me with dire consequences should they appear in this book. Somehow I have managed to sneak them in without their knowledge. I'll deal with what they do to me later. And my late father whose shirt tails I would hang on to as he made his way through the market, advising all his friends there on subjects as practical as their insurance needs to subjects as loose as their morals – to all of them I am deeply grateful. For their unstinting love and for the stories.